My Troubles

Ten cozy tales of mystery and murder

Molly MacRae

My Troubles

All rights reserved

These are works of fiction. Any resemblance between events, places, or characters, within them, and actual events, organizations, or people, is but happenstance.

No part of this book may be reproduced or transmitted in any form or by any means, electronic or mechanical, including photocopying, recording, or by any information storage and retrieval system, without permission in writing from the publisher.

Center cover illustration © 2000 by Hank Blaustein

Several of these stories and the cover art were first published by Alfred Hitchcock Mystery Magazine.

Sample chapter of Lawn Order was previously published in 2010 by Five Star Publishing, a part of Gale, Cengage Learning.

Sample chapter of Wilder Rumors was previously published in 2007 by Five Star, a part of Thomson Gale, part of The Thomson Corporation.

Copyright © 2014 by Molly MacRae

ISBN 978-0-9908428-7-3

Published December, 2014

Published in the United States of America

Darkhouse Books

160 J Street, #2223

Niles, California 94539

The Stories

My Trouble	5
Speaking Terms	11
Missing Something	21
Ah, Paradise	33
No Can Do	53
It Takes Two	75
Fandango by Flashlight	91
Practically Perfect	107
Being Julia	127
Judging Others	145
Lawn Order (sample chapter)	157
Wilder Rumors (sample chapter)	167

Introductory text
Copyright © 2014, by Molly MacRae
My Trouble
Copyright © 1990 by Molly MacRae
First published in Alfred Hitchcock Mystery Magazine
Speaking Terms
Copyright © 1991 by Molly MacRae
First published in Alfred Hitchcock Mystery Magazine
Missing Something
Copyright © 2000 by Molly MacRae
First published in Alfred Hitchcock Mystery Magazine
Ah, Paradise
Copyright © 2000 by Molly MacRae
First published in Alfred Hitchcock Mystery Magazine
No Can Do
Copyright © 2001 by Molly MacRae
First published in Alfred Hitchcock Mystery Magazine
It Takes Two
Copyright © 2002 by Molly MacRae
First published in Alfred Hitchcock Mystery Magazine
Fandango by Flashlight
Copyright © 2005 by Molly MacRae
First published in Alfred Hitchcock Mystery Magazine
Practically Perfect
Copyright © 2014 by Molly MacRae
Being Julie
Copyright © 2014 by Molly MacRae
Judging Others
Copyright © 2014 by Molly MacRae
Lawn Order sample chapter
Copyright © 2014 by Molly MacRae
Wilder Rumors sample chapter
Copyright © 2014 by Molly MacRae

All characters appearing in this work are fictitious. Any resemblance to real persons, living or dead, is purely coincidental.

This was my first published short story, and I am forever grateful to the late Kathleen Jordan, then editor of Alfred Hitchcock Mystery Magazine, for accepting it. The idea for the story came to me when I'd brought my mother's ashes home to await burial in the spring. Having her "with" me was oddly comforting, but also... odd. So I asked myself "what if?" My Trouble was the answer.

First published in Alfred Hitchcock Mystery Magazine, January 1990.

My Trouble

My mother came to live with me in November. Which is really only interesting if you consider that she died in October. No, she isn't a ghost. I'm not haunted. Give me some credit, we aren't that sort of people.

She's in the closet on the shelf. You know, it's funny, I'd never realized how heavy the cremains of a 180-pound woman would be. She's in a neat, shiny, brown plastic box about the size of an economy-size Kleenex box. It's pretty hefty. It's sealed, otherwise I suppose accidents might happen. One of the cats could get up there and push it off the shelf, for instance, and it would fall and open up and all hell would break loose, figuratively speaking, and possibly literally speaking depending on where..., oh, well, never mind.

My sister, Bitsy, (we are that sort of people, I'm afraid) wanted to keep Mother at her house until all the far-flung relatives meet down in Georgia for the burial this summer. She couldn't handle it, though. She and Mother were very close and it bothered Bitsy to have that trivial looking brown plastic reminder of her in the house. She would rather contemplate Mother serenely floating somewhere in the spiritual hereafter, than sitting someplace where she might have to shove her aside to find the extra vacuum cleaner bags.

Bitsy, needless to say, thinks I'm crass for treating Mother's presence with such nonchalance. I don't. It's just that at last I can relax, because I finally know exactly where Mother is and what she isn't doing.

She isn't, for instance, sitting on the sofa telling me that I ought to lose weight. In fact, I think I'll have another cookie right now, excuse me while I go get one.

She also isn't explaining to me how I should be using my MBA for something other than running a second-hand bookstore. That the second-hand books I deal in are usually first editions and often rare, cost the earth and usually fetch it, didn't, to her mind, make up for the fact that I sell used merchandise and operate out of my living room. Once, when I got wind of one of her infrequent and always unannounced visits, I screwed a red light bulb into the porch light. I'm sure it only served to cement her convictions.

"Your mother never really did much for you, did she?" That was my mother's cousin meowing over the garden fence soon after Mother's death. "She was always coming down on you in favor of Bitsy."

"Well, now, Leona," I tried to pour oil on these acrid waters. "I wouldn't go so far as to say that."

"And that's your trouble," snapped Leona and tottered away on her 75 year-old toothpicks.

I snapped off the dead head of a rose and stared after her. Leona was probably right. Mother's presence in my life was no great windfall. But I've never dwelt on that, and I don't think my lack of publicly aired grievances is my trouble.

Leona sounds like it, but she really isn't a nasty old lady. She just tries to improve me by telling me what my trouble is. She pinpoints a new one every so often, though she's most fond of telling me that I don't smile or laugh often enough.

My Trouble

Actually my most immediate trouble was finding a ride to the opening of an acquaintance's new restaurant over in the next town. My car was in quarantine suffering from some near fatal fuel pump/warp speed function failure or something.

I thought Bitsy and her husband, Rodney, might like to go and so I called and asked her over for a cup of coffee. You can't just ask Bitsy a favor, you have to approach her the right way.

"Oh, no, no, no, I don't think so, Margaret. You certainly aren't going are you? You are! I can tell by the way you're trying not to blush. Margaret, Mother died only last month."

"I know, Bitsy. But I think it would be good for all of us and it would be nice to help make the opening a success. We could just make an appearance."

Bitsy started fiddling with her rings, something she does when she's aggravated. She slips them off and puts them down and then slips them back on again, over and over. It drives me crazy. I could see my cause was already lost so I decided to aggravate her a bit more.

"You could just be yourself, you wouldn't even have to have fun."

She slammed her rings back on and arranged her face to show me that she was not amused. "Why don't you go with your friend what's-his-name?"

She knew why I didn't want to go with what's-his-name, whose name is Gene. Gene is my very dear friend who has a Lamborghini and a drinking problem. It's hard to believe that the two coexist for one person, but Gene is responsible enough to know when he's had enough, and he never drives his jewel drunk. He also never lets anyone else drive it even if they are sober.

I try not to encourage Gene to go places where he'll fail. It means we sometimes don't go places together, though we often end up there together. He doesn't need my encouragement.

"Why don't you get Gene to drive you?" Bitsy is offended by any sort of moral failing. She left and went next door to call on Leona. I can guess what they had to talk about.

Gene called later that morning while I was checking through a newly arrived collection of W.W. Jacobs first editions.

"How's your car?" He had driven me home when I'd had to leave it in intensive care.

"If it doesn't respond soon I might have to consider euthanasia."

"Well, don't despair, I've got great news for you. I've got strep throat."

"That's wonderful. Why are we thrilled?"

"I'm on penicillin. No drinking."

This is true. Gene is an amazing drunk. He won't stop because his doctor or his mother or I ask him to, but he'll read on a bottle of penicillin that drugs and alcohol shouldn't be mixed so he quits drinking for the duration. You figure it out. Anyway, that was fine and we made glorious plans. He would wear his tweed jacket with the penicillin in his pocket. I would wear my small black, an outfit so-called because, though I look stunning in it, it is on the snug side.

Then Bitsy phoned to ask if she had left her rings behind on the kitchen table. I said no, because she hadn't.

"Margaret, are you sure?" That question doesn't sound like what it really was. In fact, it was a thinly veiled accusation suggesting that I might have found the rings and kept them. I'm very sensitive about that sort of thing. When I was a child I did pick up pretty things that caught my eye. Then I was caught. I was about seven, I guess, and I've yet to live it down.

"Margaret?"

There isn't any satisfying answer for that kind of question. I've found the plain and simple ones are best. "No, Bitsy."

Bitsy came over to check for herself. I met her at the door, I in my small black and she in a snit.

"Margaret, I can't imagine what has happened to my rings."

"Neither can I." Gene drove up at that point and you could see her thoughts tripping over each other trying to take in the implications of my outfit and Gene's appearance.

"Do you have another ride home?"
Plain and simple. "No."
"Is he going to let you drive?"
"No."
"Well, you're certainly not going to let him drive after he's gotten drunk, are you?"
"When he's had too much he spends the night."
"And what are you going ... then you're going to spend ..."
Her indignity went into hyper-drive and she started to splutter. I enjoyed this display of her outraged sensibilities so much that I just left her thinking what she would and climbed in beside Gene. He honked a merry goodbye that made her jump.

The opening couldn't have been lovelier. The food was delicious and my small black got smaller yet. There was live piano music and impromptu singing. But damn, if I didn't get a boiling headache. Gene was gallant and drove me home, promising to call in the morning to see how I was doing.

I always leave one or two low watt lights burning at night. I operate on the theory that one doesn't hear strange noises if it isn't dark. I was in the bathroom swallowing a couple of industrial grade aspirin when that theory was blown right out of the water. Someone was in the living room.

I'd locked the doors. I know I'd done that because I always do that because I'm very careful about doing that because I am mortally terrified of the dark and all things associated with it like people breaking into my house at night.

Footsteps were coming towards the bedroom.

I slipped quietly from the bathroom into the closet, hoping that my small black would help me blend right into the corner. I could just barely, over the sound of my heart crashing around in my throat, hear someone rummaging through the drawers of my desk and then my bureau.

The closet door started to open.

I'm good at assessing a situation with lightning speed and coming up the appropriate solution. I reached over my head and grabbed from the shelf the first heavy box my hand touched and I brought that sucker down hard.

I was standing there still feeling stunned when two policemen arrived. Leona was behind them.

"It's a good thing I put the cat out when I did. I saw someone crawling in through your kitchen window and called the police. That's your trouble. You should have a burglar alarm. Who is it, anyway?"

Bitsy sat up, moaning and holding her head.

"Did this woman break into your house, ma'am?"

"I think maybe there's been a mistake, officer."

Leona helped Bitsy to sit up on the bed. The police looked askance at the three of us and left.

"By the way, Bitsy, you left these on my coffee table." Leona dug around in her apron pocket and produced Bitsy's rings. Bitsy moaned again. She grabbed the rings and ran out the front door. Leona and I watched her go.

"What did you hit her with, anyway?"

I looked down at my hand. I was still holding the box. Leona looked at.

"Hmph. The first time your mother's come down on Bitsy in favor of you." And she stalked away.

I went back to the bathroom and took a couple more aspirin. I brushed my teeth. I put on my pajamas. I crawled under the covers. And I laughed myself to sleep.

Old Geezer, the cat in Speaking Terms, is modeled after a gray tom we had when I was a child. He was a neighborly cat with some of the same interesting habits as Old Geezer.

First published in Alfred Hitchcock Mystery Magazine, April 1991.

Speaking Terms

My sister Bitsy and I were on speaking terms. Which was a shame, because speaking with Bitsy takes up so much of my time. She can't confine herself to the basics of any single conversation. She has to back and fill and digress and impress and after awhile I would just rather be doing something else, cleaning the cat pan for instance.

Bitsy came around one morning and threw herself down at the kitchen table, flushed and breathing erratically, but without a strand of hair askew or an eyelash smudged. I ran my fingers through my own as-yet uncombed tendrils and handed her a cup of coffee in a mug sporting the slogan "Eat More Possum." Bitsy didn't notice and so I knew she was in a bad way and my morning was probably shot.

"Margaret! I've had the most hellish experience!" Bitsy has a rather shrill voice and she speaks with exclamation points. "All the goldfish are gone from our lily pond!" She paused for breath, then blinked at me. "Oh, Margaret, you're not dressed yet."

"No." I try to keep my end of these conversations short.

"But, my goodness, it's ten o'clock."

"I know."

"Well aren't you afraid someone will drop by without calling first and see you like that?"

I looked at her pointedly but the irony of what she'd said was lost on her.

"I should think your business would suffer," she streamed on. "Surely even people who buy used books expect a certain amount of decorum, even if you aren't upscale with one of those cute little shops downtown. The one on the corner of Maple and Goodwin is for rent, by the way. I mean, a conservative suit or a sensible shirtwaist in a subdued paisley might attract..."

"What does Rodney say?" I like to deflect her before she really gets going about my business, which I figure is none of her business.

"Well Rodney went to that Dress for Success seminar...."

"No, Bitsy, about the fish."

Her face crumpled and she wailed: "Rodney is the one who did it!" Then she pulled a handkerchief out of her sleeve, waved it vaguely about and blew her nose delicately into it. I was fascinated. Where does she pick up these gestures?

"Rodney killed the fish?" I asked, staring at her. This was also fascinating. I'd never thought of Bitsy's rotund husband as anything more than an insurance salesman. Had he stalked the fish relentlessly and dragged them out of the pond one by one, leaving them to gasp and gargle on the lawn? Or had he slyly poisoned them all in one mad second of abandon? The mind boggled.

"Well, Bitsy," I pitched my voice low, trying to sound solemn and concerned. She is, after all, my sister. "What exactly happened?" But I kept picturing fat Rodney, furtively casing the fishpond.

"They've been disappearing a few at a time," she hiccuped. "Every morning I go out and ring my little brass bell to let them know I'm coming to feed them. I trained them to do that myself. It's the way the Japanese do, you know, with their Koi. And the fish all come up blowing little bubbles, only every morning now more and more of them have been missing and this morning they're all gone!" Bitsy cried, then, because she is very sensitive. Which is a kind way of putting it.

And I sat wondering what this meant for the future of her marriage and for the future of my spare room.

"What are you going to do?" I finally asked, not without some unease.

"Oh, I don't know." She shuddered dramatically. "Oh, I just don't, well, I just don't think I could bear going home at this point!"

"Cousin Leona has that lovely guest room," I said.

"No! I couldn't possibly stay with Leona! She has that house so crowded with dusty frou-frou and all she ever talks about are those damned African violets of hers. Do you really think she won that first prize ribbon or did she pick it up at a garage sale?"

I'd forgotten that Bitsy and our elderly cousin were not on speaking terms. Something to do with a falling out at the Garden Club Flower Show.

"Bitsy, maybe it was some dumb kids playing a nasty joke who took the fish out of the pond."

"No, Margaret. You know very well the only children in the neighborhood are toddlers (she actually refers to small children as toddlers) and we have that six foot privacy fence around the backyard."

"But, think about it, Bitsy, why would Rodney kill the fish?"

"I think Rodney has always hated that goldfish pond," she wailed.

"Oh." Then I thought of something else. "Has Rodney been gardening lately?" I asked.

"What has that got to do with anything?" she sniffled.

"Fish make great fertilizer."

"Oh, Margaret! How can you be so unfeeling?" But I could see that something had occurred to her. Her mouth snapped shut and her eyes narrowed.

Bitsy's mind at work is an unnerving sight so I got up to make another pot of coffee. Then, being not as insensitive as I wish I sometimes were, I offered Bitsy the spare room.

"Oh, Margaret, you're sure you don't mind?" But she was already arranging herself more comfortably and putting her sweater proprietarily over the back of the chair.

"No. I'll just have to move a few books around in there." I wondered if I could move them around enough to find the bed in there. I make a reasonable living dealing in used and rare books and my inventory has grown to the point that books have spilled over into most of the rooms of my small house. I know where all the books are, it's the furniture underneath I sometimes can't locate.

"Make yourself at home this evening. Gene's coming by. We thought we'd go see a movie," I said.

"Well, I'm sure if you explain it to him he'll understand why you can't go."

"What?" I stopped sloshing water around in the sink, not sure I'd heard that quite right.

"You can't leave me alone! I need someone to talk to! What if Rodney comes by looking for me?"

"Oh, Bitsy."

"Margaret!"

Oh, Hell.

A scratching noise came at the screen door. The door opened and banged shut again. Bitsy looked around to see who had come in, but missed him, because he's short, being only an average-size cat. When she turned back to the table he was standing on it looking her in the eye.

"Yeee!" she screeched, upsetting the poor old guy. He jumped back and put his foot in her coffee cup. Luckily the coffee was cold by then or he might have flung it in her face.

"What a horrible looking cat! How did it get in? Get it off the table! You'll have to sterilize the cup!" she said.

The cat turned his back on her and proceeded to bathe himself in the middle of the table. I opened the refrigerator. He stopped mid-lick and hopped down for his breakfast.

"He's a stray," I said. "His name is Old Geezer."

"He looks diseased. Some of his fur is missing. His ears are flat. And why is he all wet, it isn't even raining."

Have I mentioned that Bitsy doesn't like cats?

I don't make a point of defending myself or anyone else to Bitsy, but Old Geezer couldn't begin to do it for himself, not with her attitude.

"He's old, Bitsy. He looks on this as his retirement home. His legs are wet because there's dew on the grass."

She swiveled around to peer at the backyard. Her lips thinned at the sight of grass unmown for several weeks. "Is your mower broken?" she asked tightly.

"No." I could have told her that I'm slothful and not mowing the grass goes along with not being dressed by 10 AM and pandering to frowzy fleabags. But Bitsy hates it when I'm honest about myself before she is.

"If that cat can let itself in how do you keep it out?" she asked.

"I don't."

Then Gene dropped in. Bitsy likes Gene as much as unmown grass or cats. She must see some cosmic connection between them. I could make a guess that what she finds detestable in all three is their unpredictability. To her, that is a moral fault. Bitsy needs consistency and routine. The unexpected is unpleasant and unwanted. Where I see a mass of delicate wildflowers drifting through my yard, she sees unkempt grass and weeds. Where a cat sees a dust mote that needs wrestling to the ground and all over the living room furniture, she sees disruption and unnecessary commotion. Where Gene saw the chance to rid himself of a high-pressure job designing big buildings he hated, she saw self-destruction and personal failure.

"Oh, hi, Bitsy." The smile on Gene's face deflated a little when he saw her. "How are you?"

"My fish were killed!" she snapped, glaring at him as though he were a conspirator in their deaths.

I think Gene visibly jumped back, though not as dramatically as Geezer had when Bitsy first addressed him. "Gee," he said, "I'm sorry."

"Bitsy thinks Rodney did it," I said.

"No kidding, Rodney?" Gene came over and put his arm around my shoulders and gave me a good morning peck on the cheek.

"Well," said Bitsy. "I see you two have other things on your mind. I will go across and speak to Cousin Leona."

"Really?" Ever hopeful me.

"Something has occurred to me, Margaret, and I'm going to take a closer look at those African violets of hers. They've been looking particularly healthy lately." She gave wide berth to Old Geezer, then stopped and looked from the cat to Gene. Geezer had beached himself on the rag rug in front of the stove and was scratching a flea. Gene was leaning against the counter, one hand vaguely rubbing his beard.

"You like cats, don't you, Gene?" she asked.

"Yes, I do," Gene replied.

"Well, Margaret, that solves that problem. Gene can take the *cat* to the movies this evening." She sailed on past and out the front door.

We listened for the purposeful slam, which accompanies Bitsy's exits. Then I told Gene about the change in our evening's plans and how understanding Bitsy was sure he would be about it. Which he wasn't particularly until I pointed out that she wasn't here now and I was. So we focused on that bright spot in our lives for awhile after which Gene straggled off to work with more than a twinkle in his eye and I opened my doors to the new business day.

Bitsy arrived back sometime shortly after noon. I told her there was tuna fish for sandwiches in the refrigerator. It was an unfortunate suggestion from her point of view, but it did stifle conversation.

She ate peanut butter and sat, her eyes fixed on the square of lawn visible through the kitchen window, muttering to herself. I caught the word "bats" but nothing more. Muttering "bats" after a chat with Cousin Leona isn't extraordinary, and though maybe I should have asked Bitsy how it had gone, I didn't have several hours to kill.

I went back to work, locating Thurber's *The Thirteen Clocks* for somebody's grandmother, selling *The Happy Hollister's and the Whistle Pig Mystery* to two small boys and in between packing a box with half a dozen P.G. Wodehouse first editions for shipment to a customer in Michigan. Then, before I forgot, I went to excavate the bed in the spare room, being careful not to confuse my sophisticated retrieval system.

The lawn mower started up. Glancing out the window I saw Bitsy attacking the backyard. From the look on her face she was a woman with a mission. I left her to it.

I can't say I didn't enjoy my evening with Bitsy. We made popcorn and sat at either end of the sofa, facing each other, eating it out of big bowls and laughing, something we hadn't done together since we were teenagers. We hadn't done it often then, either. Her bout with the backyard had left her in good spirits, probably deluding her into thinking she was making progress towards her life-long goal of setting me straight. I saw no harm in letting her dream on.

She even kept her feet up on the sofa when Gene showed up with "Bringing Up Baby" on tape and sat down between us. I think she was encouraged because he didn't bring a six-pack with him and he kept his shoes on.

Then Rodney arrived. Bitsy's mouth got small. She stood up so she could turn her back on him.

"Evening, Gene, Margaret," said Rodney. He pulled a handkerchief out of his sans-a-belt pocket and wiped his forehead. He took several deep breaths. He studied the floor in front of his toes, which came into view just beyond the edge of his belly. Then he raised his head and pursed his lips momentarily before speaking to his wife.

He was masterful. I hadn't known what it takes to make an insurance salesman. But Rodney has it. And it worked on Bitsy. Within minutes they were clinging to each other, the near-wreckage of their wedded bliss sweeping past, forgotten.

"Oh, Rodney, I knew it couldn't be you," Bitsy sniffled into his shoulder. "Margaret must be right, it must have been some nasty children."

"That's alright, Honey Pot. You know I like watching you feed the little critters. In fact, I bought you some more. They're not very big, yet, but they'll grow. There's the prettiest little orange fantail with white spots, and a couple of those gold pop-eyes you like. You come on home now and give them names."

"Oh, Rodney."

They spooned their way out the front door. Gene and I followed and we all stood on the porch in the mellow light of the moon while Bitsy went on saying goodbye. Someone should have taken a picture then, of the four of us standing there exuding warmth, companionship, pleasure, and used it as an advertisement for some cozy beverage, or saved it for five or ten minutes to give us a few laughs after what happened next.

As we smiled and the men shook hands again and Bitsy was saying something about artichoke hearts, Old Geezer trotted up the front steps. He dropped a small parcel on Gene's shoe and gave his old cat's version of a mew.

The crickets ceased to chirp. Ourselves silent, as one, we bent forward, to stare at Gene's foot. We focused on the orange body with fantail and white spots nestled there on his laces. Bitsy was the only one to comment.

"YEEeeee!" she said.

Geezer leaped straight up into Gene's arms and clung there, appalled.

Between finger and thumb, Rodney picked up the fish. He held it up and looked from Gene to me to Old Geezer, who had calmed slightly and was shaking, one by one, his wet legs.

"Margaret!" shrieked Bitsy. "I...."

I cut her off. "I think Gene and Geezer make a handsome couple, don't you?"

"They'd better make it a permanent arrangement!" she snapped. And she and Rodney stalked off into the night.

Leona tottered over from next door while Gene and Geezer were getting into Gene's car.

"Was that Bitsy who just left?" she asked.

"Mmm," I answered.

"I've got something for her." She produced a plastic bag from her apron pocket. "It's bat guano," she said. "I use it on my African violets. Thought she might like some, but the way she rushed out muttering this afternoon I didn't have a chance to give it to her. What's Gene doing with that cat?"

Gene was trying to get Old Geezer to sit down in the passenger seat of his beautiful dark blue Lamborghini. Geezer wanted to stand in the driver's seat with his paws on the steering wheel.

"They look good together," said Leona. "They both have a moth-eaten look about them, but they look damned handsome in that car."

"You're right," I said.

"You should spend more time with him," she said, looking at me slyly. "I like him. How about giving Bitsy this bat guano next time you see her. She isn't speaking to me, apparently."

"Actually, Cousin Leona, I don't think she's speaking to me right now, either."

Leona looked back at Gene who was still explaining things to the cat.

"Hmph. You've got time on your hands, then. Good night, dear."

She gave me a little push towards the car. She stayed to wave as the three of us drove off.

A story of too much zucchini and failing memory. I wrote this story right after my father "lost" his truck. He and I found the truck – around the corner where he'd parked it – but that was the day I realized I was beginning to lose him.

First published in Alfred Hitchcock Mystery Magazine, May 2000.

Missing Something

My cousin Leona turns 80 next month. Which isn't especially old, but she's beginning to forget things. She's getting 'whiffy' as we politely say in our family. Most of her whiffiness shows in little ways that don't really make much difference. Like she told me three times yesterday that the Garden Club is meeting at her house next week. She won't forget the meeting, she just probably won't remember not to tell me about it a few more times. And ask me if I'll be there. Which I won't because I'm not and never have been a member of the Garden Club. But that's okay, that doesn't really bother me. What I worry about is when she'll start leaving the water running or forgetting to turn a burner off on the stove. There's precedent for that among my older relatives. That seems to be the way we go in our family.

My sister, Bitsy, and I approach our worries from different directions. That's the way it always goes in our family.

"Margaret, you turn everything into a joke or a funny story." That was Bitsy, appalled on the phone, when I told her about Cousin Leona trying to remember which of us was older, Bitsy or I. I had told Leona that I was definitely the taller and that was all that mattered. I shouldn't have told Bitsy. What she lacks in height she doesn't make up for in a sense of humor.

"And it's not as though half an inch makes any difference, anyway," said Bitsy, getting in the last word before slamming down the receiver. Well, for some of us it obviously does.

Bitsy takes a militaristic approach to the worries of Leona's old age. She's manning her mental barricades. She's fending off the potential sapping of her own cerebral powers with a self-improvement regimen that involves some complicated equation of bottled mineral water, organic vegetables and attacking every corner of her life with a very chic new-age spiritual panacea. She's added the further complication of insisting on yet another attempt in her life-long quest to get me to shape up. And that's where my little self-improvement effort comes in. While Bitsy improves herself via the vegetation/meditation/irrigation route, I'm making an effort to improve myself by not disparaging Bitsy's efforts. Or strangling her.

Cousin Leona lives next door to me. She is actually my late mother's cousin, which makes her a second or once removed or something I've never bothered to be entirely clear on. Dear Abby could set me straight. Bitsy could, too, but I don't think I'll call her right now and ask her. Leona's house is crowded with the African violets she dotes on the way some people do small dogs or precocious grandchildren. She can't abide either of those mild plagues and Bitsy and I get as tired of hearing about her violets as we would micro dogs or grandchildren. But between the three of us we actually cope pretty well within the strained bonds of familial relationship. I picture us as connected by three rubber bands. Sometimes we're loose and comfortable with each other and sometimes we're a little stretched. Someday I wonder if I might snap altogether but so far so good.

Leona has taken to tottering over to my house sometime around the middle of each morning. My place is crowded with books. I've turned it into the dream so many people have of running a bookstore in a lovely old house. The reality is that living at work can be hell, but what the hell, it's mine and I like it.

If I can stop what I'm doing I usually make Leona a cup of tea. Otherwise she totters back out again and goes about her little old lady business.

This morning Leona and Bitsy arrived together.

"Margaret, I've brought you a surprise," said Bitsy in her endearingly aggressive way. "Here."

"Well, gosh, Bitsy. Thanks. Leona, would you like a slice of...?"

"It's zucchini biscotti. And it's for your customers," Bitsy said, taking the plate back from my hand and looking around for a place to put it. "I think it would be a great idea if you started serving coffee and little nibbles. You know all the big bookstores do."

"Thank you, Bitsy," I said between quietly gnashing teeth. "I do know."

"Oh, and I have plenty of extra zucchini. Would you like some?"

"No! No, that's all right Bitsy." She's convinced that her evening meditations in the zucchini football field she planted is what accounts for the superabundance of squash now gracing every flat surface in her house.

"Well! You know, Margaret, it wouldn't hurt you to eat more fresh vegetables!"

"Bitsy, please, not now."

Her mouth screwed up tight and her eyes took on a gimlet glare. I braced myself for a blast.

But something amazing happened. Bitsy closed her eyes. She took a deep breath, held it for several counts, and then let it out again, slowly and evenly, with a peaceful little sigh.

"That's fine, that's fine. Margaret, I'll just nip into the kitchen and start a pot of coffee to go with the biscotti. This is my gift to you. I'm happy to share my ideas with you." And with that, she turned and floated out of the room.

"Wow," I said to Leona as we stared at her retreating back. "She was..."

"Serene," said Leona. "I think she's growing as a person. Margaret dear, I know you're usually the first to loathe admitting that Bitsy is right about anything, but this nibble idea has merit."

"Yeah, yeah, I know." I, too, can show personal growth. "In fact, what would really be good, is if I made samples from recipes in some of the new cookbooks."

"Or magazines, dear. There happens to be a recipe for zucchini biscotti in the latest Herb Life. Now, do you need anything from the garden center? Bone meal for your bulbs?"

I don't have any bulbs.

"No, thanks, Cousin Leona. My bone meal level is fine. I'll see you later."

I cleared space for the plate of biscotti on the counter near the cash register. Then to show further evidence of personal growth and to give Bitsy her due I added a little sign saying, "have a bite of Bitsy's biscotti." It was too cute, but even personal growth can have its downside.

Bitsy returned with the coffee in an insulated carafe. She looks unnervingly like her role model, June Cleaver, sometimes. Last year for Christmas I made her a sweatshirt with WWJCD on the front and a picture of June on the back. I've haven't seen it since.

But Bitsy beamed at the sign and put the coffee next to the plate.

"Cups?" she asked brightly.

"I'll rustle some up. Thanks, Bitsy, this'll be great."

"Bye!" she chirruped, and was gone. Amazing.

I really could get into this I thought as I absentmindedly ate another piece of the zucchini biscotti. Then I caught sight of my reflection in the glass of the front door and sadly realized another downside to personal growth. It obviously works both figuratively and literally and my figure would literally go up a dress size a week if I ate all the samples myself. So, standing across the room from the plate on the counter, I started leafing through the low-fat no-fat cookbooks, trying not to gain weight just from smelling the ink.

Between the customers who wandered in out of the glorious summer sunshine, and drooling through recipes I would either be crazy to attempt or crazy to tempt myself with, the morning passed pleasantly enough. I even sold several copies of Herb Life with the zucchini biscotti recipe. But I couldn't shake the image of Bitsy, serene. The vision of her marshaling her emotions like that kept replaying in my mind and I couldn't stop shaking my head over it. Was I missing something? Bitsy has lived her entire life in bold Italics, her every statement highlighted in florescent pink. Could this be zucchini serenity? Maybe I should start browsing the bottled water aisle at the grocery. Still, Bitsy's serenity would have to linger a little longer before I asked to borrow her meditation tapes.

Along about noon Leona called.

"Margaret, dear, I'm sorry to bother you when I know you're so busy."

"That's all right, Cousin Leona, what's up?"

"It's the strangest thing. I can't find my car. I think maybe it's been stolen."

"You're kidding! Where are you?" I asked.

"Well, I went to the garden center and got a few things I needed. Oh, and two bags of that bone meal you wanted because it was on sale. Then I thought I'd stop by the mall. You know I really do hate the way traffic zips around out there, but the Senior Citizen Task Force is doing their free cholesterol screenings and I like to support them. And I parked outside Penney's, because that's where I always do, but now it's not there."

"Are you sure you didn't park it somewhere else?"

There was an uncomfortable pause. Keen though Leona has always been to remind me of anything three or more times, she is sensitive about her own failing memory.

"Did you talk to the mall security people?" I asked contritely.

"I didn't like to bother them, dear. And I didn't want them thinking I'm just a batty old lady."

My mother raised me better than to say something at this point.

"I did try calling Bitsy, dear, because I know you have the shop to run. But she's not home."

Figures.

"Cousin Leona, could you take a taxi home? I can't leave the store right now, but later this afternoon I'll take you back there and we'll look around. For clues. Or something." Her car is one of those nice, sensible, compact jobs that looks like two hundred other cars in any given parking lot. And there are usually five hundred more that you can eventually pick out as not yours only because they're really some other nondescript shade of the same metallic finish. I was willing to bet her car was out there.

"Well...." She sounded dubious.

"If we don't find anything we'll report it stolen." Leona likes real policemen.

"All right, then, dear. Thank you. I'll see you later."

Swell. I wondered where Bitsy was. Off spreading benevolence and serenity somewhere, no doubt. I realized I was glaring at the zucchini biscotti. It was only a barely adequate Bitsy substitute, though, so I turned my back on it in a huff and went to the kitchen to eat lunch.

That's where I discovered what Bitsy was really up to. Spreading zucchini. There was a small mountain of it on my kitchen table. I knew I'd missed something this morning while Bitsy did her serene zucchini queen bit. I'd missed her extra large handbag. And her sneakiness. Damn.

I didn't make a zucchini sandwich for lunch or a zucchini anything else, and after enjoying that fact and several hundred fat laden calories I felt better. I was even jolly when one of the customers who'd bought a copy of Herb Life this morning brought it back saying the recipe for zucchini biscotti had been torn out.

These things happen sometimes, so I gave her an intact copy and she left smiling.

It was hard to be as blithe when a copy of Vegetarian News was returned later with several pages ripped out. And although I tried not to let the customer see it, when a copy of Bountiful Garden came back with a page of recipes missing, I was hard pressed not to be downright cranky.

I'm naturally suspicious. Along with being sarcastic it's one of my more winning traits. So when I looked to see exactly what recipes were missing from the magazines, I wasn't, somehow, surprised. Zucchini marmalade. Zucchini tofutti. Zucchini chow chow. Zucchini panini.

An obvious solution to the mystery of the missing recipes was that Bitsy, in some kind of zucchini haze, had come searching for more ways to deal with her overabundance. But I couldn't believe that. Bitsy might lead her life on the marginal line and she fairly regularly crushes my joie de vivre under the heels of her pointy shoes, but the beauty of Bitsy is that she is predictable and she doesn't really set out to be destructive. Still, having so recently experienced an alien vegetable encounter in my kitchen, I wondered. I know if I had that much zucchini lurking in the underbrush I'd be tempted to take desperate measures.

I wanted to talk to her about Cousin Leona, anyway, and, as I don't usually shrink from a little Bitsy baiting, I called and left a message on her machine that she couldn't refuse.

"Margaret! " she later blared into the phone that I hadn't gotten far enough from my ear for auditory health or comfort before realizing it was her calling back. "Of course I have more biscotti! I'll bring it right over!" She was delighted. I could tell. I rubbed my ear and thought of a cunning and safe way of finding out if she was systematically vandalizing my magazine stand.

"Margaret, don't be ridiculous. Zucchini tofutti sounds repulsive! Can you imagine what color it would be?"

Good old reliable Bitsy. How could I ever have imagined she would even look at such a gauche recipe? Thank goodness I'd only had the bad taste to ask if she'd heard of the stuff and hadn't actually asked her to share a recipe for it. Her reaction was everything I'd hoped for and expected. I still didn't know who was pilfering recipes, but it was comforting knowing that Bitsy's zucchini fetish hadn't dulled either her morals or her sense of style.

Her sensitivity towards anyone else's infirmity was another story.

"Bitsy, have you talked to Leona this afternoon?"

"No. I noticed her car's gone, though. She must be out and about somewhere."

"Actually, she says her car is missing."

"What?"

"Well, she thinks maybe it was stolen."

"She didn't lock it, did she? Do you know how many times I've warned her about that? I've told her over and over!"

And over and over.

"I even threatened to have Rodney drop her insurance!"

Rodney is Bitsy's husband. He's an insurance agent. Threatening Leona with Rodney's wrath would be like menacing her with a comfortably worn teddy bear decked out in sans-a-belt golf clothes. A nerve-wracking experience, maybe, but nothing she couldn't laugh about later.

"Bitsy, I think she just doesn't remember where she parked it. I'll take her over to the mall later and I'm sure we'll find it. But I'm getting worried. I think we're going to have to start thinking about not letting her drive anymore."

"Why? She isn't dangerous. She never goes over 20 miles an hour. What I'm doing is eating brain-building foods. It's probably too late for Leona, but you should try it and at least she could be taking those memory supplements."

"Gecko Baboon Oil?"

"Margaret! Don't joke about things you're unwilling to open your mind to. How did Leona get home? And why didn't she call me?"

"You weren't home. She hates your machine."

"Well!"

"Calm down, Bitsy. Remember, be one with the Great Zucchini." She looked like she could personally steam my zucchini.

And then it happened again. I saw it with my own eyes and was transfixed. Her prim little pucker receded into a smile. Lightening stopped shooting out of her fingertips. Her hair relaxed.

"I'm sure you will find her car," she practically hummed. "And think about this, Margaret, if you remember where you were when you leave something, then you haven't lost it."

That's when I lost it.

"What the hell does that mean?"

"Margaret, you don't need to swear at me. I'm only helping."

"Bitsy, have you noticed, at all, that your way of helping doesn't even involve Leona? You're looking for some kind of cosmic solution that has nothing to do with the little old lady who used to tie our shoes. You're just avoiding the messiness you might find if you really looked at the situation. Your aphorisms and profound pronouncements don't mean anything to someone who can't remember where she parked her car. And they don't add anything to a conversation, either."

Once again I prove I'm adept at personal shrinkage.

Bitsy, eyes popping, left. I closed up shop for the day and slunk over to Leona's for our car finding mission.

"You look upset, dear," Leona greeted me at her door. "I'm sorry to put you to this trouble."

"Oh, no, that's all right, Leona. I was just shrieking at Bitsy and I'm feeling deflated. Do you think I'll ever learn?"

"No, but I wouldn't worry about it, dear. It's just part of you being you and Bitsy being Bitsy. You've been at it as long as I can remember. It'll blow over. It always does. And she'll enjoy forgiving you. Now, shall I drive or you?"

"I'll drive. Your car is missing, remember?"

"Is it? Of course I remember, dear. Let's go."

"Do you happen to know your license plate number?"

"I haven't bothered to remember one of those since 1960."

"I probably don't know mine, either. You just show me where you usually park and we'll see what we find."

What we found was cars all obviously cloned from a single dentless bumper, all neatly laid out in rows that undulated gently towards the horizon. A long evening loomed ahead of us.

"There, see that pretty crepe myrtle? That's the row I like to park in. But I looked and my car isn't there."

I found an empty space under the crepe myrtle and got out to reconnoiter. Leona stopped to pull a few weeds from around the crepe myrtle and then trailed after me.

"Isn't that your car next to the one with the baby seat in it?"

"I don't have a baby seat in my car."

"No, but isn't this one yours? Sure it is."

"Well, but Margaret, this car is all locked up and there's a bag of groceries in the back seat."

"That's not your stuff from the garden center?"

"I distinctly remember asking the man at the garden center to put your bags of bone meal in the trunk."

My bags of bone meal. I could see bulbs in my future. I peered into the back seat. And then I straightened back up feeling more like my old self again.

"Cousin Leona, may I have your keys?"

"Of course, dear."

I unlocked the car.

"I don't understand. I didn't lock my car."

I pulled out the bag of groceries. Zucchini.

"Bitsy did."

"Bitsy did what?"

"Locked your car for you."

"Is that her zucchini?"

"It looks like yours, now."

"Well, then it's a good thing I have all these wonderful recipes." Leona pulled a small stash of magazine clippings out of her pocket.

"Oh, Leona."

"Am I missing something, dear? Why are you laughing?"

"It's not as messy as crying. Come on, I think I'll drive both ways today. You and your zucchini hop back into my car."

"What about mine?"

"Bitsy knows where it is. I think we'll go roust her from her zucchini dreams."

I popped Leona's trunk and got my bags of bone meal.

"Cousin Leona? What kind of bulbs are your favorite?"

"Daffodils, dear. Daffies, my mother called them when she started getting whiffy."

"Daffies. That sounds about right. Will you help me plant some?"

"Of course, dear. We'll put them in next to your tulips. After the Garden Club meeting at my house next week."

"Perfect. Let's go home."

"Shall I drive or you?"

"I'll drive."

"Thank you, dear."

"If you'll tie my shoe."

"Don't be silly, Margaret."

My husband loves to fish for trout in the creeks and rivers of east Tennessee. He's a catch and release kind of guy though, so unlike poor Bitsy, I've never had to worry about freezer space.

First published in Alfred Hitchcock Mystery Magazine, November 2000.

Ah, Paradise

I didn't call the police when my sister, Bitsy, disappeared. And of course now I'm never supposed to forgive myself. Which is something of a dilemma because I'm usually the only one I can count on to do that. Long memories in my family. Long, sticky, tenacious memories that have ways of sneaking up from behind when you're least expecting them. You've read about the amazing tensile strength of a thin strand of spider silk? A single strand of unpleasant memory in my family is something like that.

But I really didn't think anything of it when Bitsy didn't call or come around for a few days. Well, actually I did think something, and that was something like 'ah, paradise'. But at this point I don't think I should go around advertising that little lapse in good taste.

And if you think about it, and I do mean you because I certainly don't want to, this is one of those stories of complicated modern life that works on several levels, each one of which can be conveniently labeled my fault. Well, at least I'm thorough.

"Margaret, I'm thoroughly fed up!" That was Bitsy, pre-disappearance, coming down the hallway toward my kitchen where I was hanging on the refrigerator door, staring in at the lack of anything worth eating. I let the door smugly pull itself closed again and very gently banged my head three times against the freezer compartment. It didn't help. No superstitious act on my part has ever kept Bitsy from my door.

She stopped and stared at me briefly. I tried to look casual, which wasn't really too hard because I was still in my pajamas.

"Margaret, why is the middle of your forehead red?" But before I could think of a snappy answer her mind had jumped back onto its single track. "Why in god's name did you ever let Rodney buy those books on bass fishing?" she cried, flinging her arms wide to emphasize the depth of her chagrin. Her decibel level alone would have done that, but the arms were a nice touch. Too bad in her exuberance she also knocked my radio into the sink with the dirty dishes.

"Oh! What was that?" she asked, looking toward the sink suspiciously.

"I think it was the end of Sir Georg Solti conducting Mozart's Symphony No. 40."

"Really? It sounded more like the middle of the piece."

"Well," I said, carefully using a pot holder to pull the plug from the outlet and then fishing the poor old radio out of the scummy water, "in this case, Bitsy, it was the end."

She looked askance at me and my radio. I think she gave a little shudder. I gave the radio a little shake and put it on a dishtowel to drain.

"So, Bitsy, what's up?"

"I am thoroughly fed up!"

"Oh. Right. You said that. Hmm." At this point I was only lending half my brain to the conversation as I used the other half to locate a pen and some paper to start a grocery list.

"Well?" Bitsy, impatient.

Ah, Paradise

I'd flubbed my lines. I turned back to her, composing my face in something I hoped looked like interest and resorted to my old reliable 'Response to Bitsy in a Crisis' line.

"Why don't you tell me all about it?"

Success. Bitsy threw herself into a chair at the table and wound herself up to wail on about her problems. Having found pen and paper, I started my list. Bananas. Crackers. Then I wondered if I was really making out a grocery list after all. I thought about adding fruitcake, but it was the wrong season.

"Margaret! I'm limping! Why are you over there sniggering?"

Obviously I'd missed something while contemplating nuts I've known and put up with. I dragged back that part of my mind that was enjoying itself and gave all my attention to Bitsy's lamentations.

"You're limping?"

"Well, you would be too, if ten pounds of frozen bass had fallen out of the freezer onto your foot."

I guess so. "What are you doing with ten pounds of frozen bass in your freezer?" I asked, genuinely curious, which surprised me.

"Thanks to you and what's his name, Rodney has gone completely loopy about fishing."

At this point I would have liked to argue the logic of her placing the blame at my doorstep, but in the interest of abbreviating my conversations with Bitsy I'm sometimes willing to absorb a certain amount of guilt. So I opted instead for another question I was actually interested in. "Hasn't he heard of catch and release?"

The look on her face was answer enough.

"How much have you got in your freezer?" I asked, shying away a little, sort of afraid of the answer.

The look on her face was answer enough. Well, I can only absorb so much guilt quietly. Bitsy had endlessly moaned about tripping over her husband every time she turned around on the weekends and how he needed to find a hobby to get him out of the house. My sometimes dear one, what's his name, whose name is Gene, suggested fishing and took him out on the lake one Saturday. And Rodney had fun. So I sold him a few books on the joys of bass fishing.

"Bitsy, I sell books. People buy books. How they react to those books is not something under my control. I sell information, education, illumination, entertainment. I don't sell sanity or insanity. The embarrassment of bass in your freezer is not my fault." She started to puff up in that peculiar way she has when she's thinking about Gene. "And it's not Gene's fault, either. He thought he was doing you a favor." So there. I turned back to my list and added Fruit Loops.

Then, because I'm not totally heartless, I thought I probably ought to show a little more concern for her foot.

"Bitsy, did you put something cold on your foot?"

"What would you suggest? Frozen fish?" she snapped. I hadn't actually thought of that and was still delighting in the vision of Bitsy's foot propped up on a stool, tucked therapeutically amidst a school of frozen largemouths when I heard the door slam behind her. Oh well. I thought of bowing three times toward the east to see if that would keep Bitsy away for awhile, but I'm not really that irrational. A stout bar nailed across the door would be more effective.

Along about midmorning, good old what's his name wandered into the bookstore, which occupies every square inch of the front half of my house. Gene and I are an on again off again item. Bitsy commented on that once, loudly, in public. Gene told her he'd noticed that, too, and the funny thing about it was that when we were on again, he more often than not found his pants off again. That's one of the reasons Bitsy likes to have trouble with his name. Gene makes her nervous. Part of his charm.

"Hello, my little bit of trout bait," he said as he nibbled my ear. It was an odd endearment considering some of the things trout eat. But he had a bag of groceries with him so I nuzzled him back.

"Are we on again for the Charity Tournament Banquet and Ball?" he asked.

I swallowed a bite of the apple I'd swiped from his bag. "When is it?"

"A week from Saturday. You can wear your small black," he said, a becoming leer stealing across his face. Gene is ever the zealous admirer of my skimpy black evening dress, made skimpier by the extra pounds I never seem able to shed.

"You don't think I'll be a little over dressed with everyone else wearing hip waders?"

"Not if that's all they're wearing."

"Oh, a classy affair, I had no idea. Funny Bitsy didn't mention the banquet this morning."

Gene shuddered at mention of Bitsy. Probably the only thing he has in common with her, they're both good shudderers.

"Ah, she was here, wasn't she? I thought my ears were burning because of too much sun. Well, Rodney bought tickets same time I did. We could probably make it a gruesome foursome."

"Oh that would be jolly. Unless she brains him first with a block of bass. She wasn't feeling overly fond of fish this morning."

"A feeling the fish reciprocate, I'm pretty sure. But she hasn't left him again and moved in with you, has she?" He looked alarmed and hopeful at the same time, an astonishing combination that showed off his blue eyes to good advantage. I gave him a smooch to soothe him.

"No, she blames you and me for Rodney's fishing affliction and I didn't offer a sympathetic enough shoulder to cry on, or an accommodating doormat in either sense of the word. She's pretty unhappy with all three of us. How much you want to bet she tries to keep him out of the tournament altogether?"

"Why?"

"Oh, who knows. Maybe he'll show some gumption for once and lock her in the fishing shack and just go without her."

"He'd have to drag her in by the heels."

That's another thing Bitsy can't quite get over about Gene. He's an architect and when he first mentioned his fishing shack she assumed he was being modest and was talking about a sweet little lakeside cottage. In fact, shack is an overly optimistic description. It's more like a fishing hovel. He's very proud of it. Bitsy, after one look, now calls it the fishing sty. Rodney is enchanted by it. I don't think he ever had a clubhouse or a tree house when he was a child. Gene doesn't think he ever was a child.

"Rodney dragging Bitsy into the fishing shack." This idea appealed to what I'm told is my immature sense of humor. "Over her dead body!" And I probably guffawed a little. Then I pulled myself together. "Well, now there's an image to haunt me the rest of the day."

I took the bag of groceries from Gene and we made plans for a movie and a canoodle that evening. He said goodbye in a spirited sort of way that left me breathless and blushing and so I went about my business day. And as it turns out I wasn't haunted at all by the image of Bitsy and the fishing shack because I'm serious when it comes to business and though bookselling is a pleasant occupation, I try not to distract myself with that much hilarity.

Tales of second sight always fascinate me. I've never believed any of them but it's such a slick idea. Knowing what's going to happen ahead of time would be a handy talent in so many areas of daily life. What I put more faith in, though, is the baloney factor. Which is why I wasn't spooked or suspicious or even particularly bothered when I started not seeing Bitsy.

But along about Thursday I did wonder just a little. I wouldn't call what I was feeling stirrings of unease, but I did wonder.

Monday her friend Barbara had come into the bookstore wondering if I knew where Bitsy was. She'd missed a Garden Club meeting.

"Oh well," said Barbara brightly. "Something must have come up. Maybe she and Rodney are taking advantage of this beautiful afternoon and are out at the lake. Hey, did you see that sweatshirt Bitsy got him?"

"No."

"It's a hoot! It says 'My wife says if I go fishing one more time she's gonna leave me! Gosh, I'm gonna miss her!' Isn't that a hoot?"

Bitsy's friends say things like hoot.

"Sure is, Barbara. I'll tell Bitsy you were looking for her. Bye!" I said brightly. Barbara is one of those people who comes into the bookstore and has never yet bought a book. Maybe she only reads sweatshirts.

Tuesday, trying to think ahead and be organized and to gain points in the Good Sister Club, I called Bitsy to see if she and Rodney wanted to go with us to the banquet. Only their answering machine was home so I passed the time of day with it and hung up.

Wednesday the bookstore did stellar business. Computers and the Internet have changed so many things forever, including the used book world. Volumes and sets of books that might have moved in and lived comfortably on my shelves for so long that I would have thought of them as freeloading relatives were now sometimes leaving before I even gave them a proper hello. Part of me is saddened by this or at least bemused. But the part of me that enjoys keeping a bank balance is content.

The day was also blessedly Bitsy-free, which is why I indulged myself by saying 'ah, paradise!' before sinking into the sofa at sundown with a cold beer.

But by Thursday, as I say, I began to wonder. Maybe I was experiencing a touch of Bitsy withdrawal. Or premature twinges of guilt for enjoying my quietude. I saw Gene at lunch and asked him if he'd seen Rodney lately.

"Not to say saw," he said. I must have slipped and given him a Bitsy-like look because he stepped back a bit and rather quickly went on to explain. "Some of the guys in the bar at the marina saw him."

This time I gave him a look and I know it wasn't just Bitsy-like. But I couldn't help myself. One of the reasons Gene and I haven't become a permanent item is his habit of stopping in bars and forgetting to leave. He sighed. I sighed. And he went on to tell me what the guys had been saying.

"He was out on the lake most of the weekend and Sunday he started really pulling in some big suckers. One of the guys, Mort, said he asked him what he was using and Rodney wouldn't tell him. Said it was his own secret formula. Actually the guys were kind of laughing about that."

"Why?"

"Well, it's kind of unlikely that a guy like Rodney would come up with anything a hundred other guys, who've all been fishing a hell of a lot longer than he has, haven't already tried."

"Hmm."

"Yeah, hmm. But he insisted this was his own formula and nothing anyone else could have come up with."

"Stranger things have happened."

"They did. Rodney made a bet with Mort that he'd win the tournament."

"Wow." Rodney is such a straight arrow, making a bet was, for him, like Bitsy asking Gene for a back rub. Highly unlikely.

"Why the interest in Rodney?"

"Oh, well, actually I was wondering about Bitsy."

"Stranger things have happened."

"Stranger than her or stranger than me wondering about her?"

He had trouble deciding that point and apparently thought nuzzling my neck would help. I only absent-mindedly returned his affection and sat vaguely stirring the potato chips around on my plate. Both these actions were sufficiently uncharacteristic of me that he took notice and, bless him, took my disquiet seriously.

"So you haven't seen her or heard from her for how long?"

"I don't know, a week? I know that's not all that long, but..."

"But we're not dealing with just anyone, we're dealing with Bitsy."

"Exactly." Bitsy can be and often is the most aggravating person. She's bossy, wheedling, meddling, controlling. She can strip paint with her voice. She doesn't like cats and she digs dandelions out of my lawn. But there is a goodness deep inside Bitsy. In trying to explain how I feel about her to Gene I once told him that if she didn't exist I would have to invent her. I need a little Bitsy in my life to give it balance. Everyone could use a little Bitsy. She's good for the soul.

"She's not answering her phone or returning your calls?"

"No."

"Did you piss her off in some way?"

"Well, that's a given, Gene, but that would also only increase the odds of her coming over here to either screech at me or say she'd forgiven me. And besides, it's not just me who hasn't seen her. She missed a Garden Club meeting Monday. Barbara came looking for her."

"Horrors." That summed up both the missed meeting and the visit from Barbara. "Call Rodney at work."

Of course. "Now why didn't I think of that?"

"You're worried."

"I am?"

"And you're not thinking straight."

I thought about that for a minute and ended up nodding my head. "Will wonders never cease."

Having settled this remarkable fact into the part of my brain where I store other notions that startle and perplex me, I returned most of my attention to my lunch, sparing the better part of it (my attention not my lunch) for Gene. Then he went back to work and I called Rodney.

Rodney is an insurance salesman. He does everything well and thoroughly and forthrightly. If Al Gore had been an insurance salesman, he would have been Rodney. Al Gore is better looking, though. Given all that, I was surprised when Rodney hemmed and hawed on the phone.

"But Rodney, she usually at least returns my messages."

"Our machine isn't working."

"Oh. Well, will she be in this evening?"

He dithered a bit more. "She's got a meeting. I think. Yeah, I'm sure. She said a meeting. Late."

"What meeting?"

"Oh, gosh, look at the time. Gotta go, Margaret. Appointment." And he hung up. I sat staring at the phone.

Friday morning Barbara stopped by the bookstore, again, disturbed over Bitsy's continued non-presence.

"It's spooky," she said. "It's like she's just vanished. Poof!"

I kept my thoughts to myself and didn't give her any solace. She didn't buy a book.

Bitsy gave me a house key once so I could go in and water her plants while she and Rodney were on vacation. She never asked me to do that again but I still have the key. I tried calling her at lunchtime on Friday and snubbed the supposedly broken machine when only it answered. Then I went over to her house and let myself in.

I don't know exactly what I was expecting to find when I opened the front door. I've been searching for clues to Bitsy's mental mechanics all my life and a quiet look around her house wasn't likely to enlighten me any further along those lines. Still.

But nothing about the living room struck me as out of the ordinary. The pillows on the sofa were all invitingly plumped. In the dining room the table looked as polished as ever and her china and glassware glistened and winked at me from the hutch. In the den there was an empty glass on an end table, but that didn't alarm me. I just stored the information away in an emergency file I keep to remind myself that Bitsy is human, too.

Then I went into the kitchen. In the kitchen I found what I'd been dreading all along I might find. Disarray. And lots of it. Dirty dishes on the counter and in the sink. Cold coffee in the pot. Three days of newspapers strewn across the kitchen table. A box of Raisin Bran, open, on top of the refrigerator. Sort of like my house but definitely not like Bitsy's.

I had to face it. Rodney was lying. Bitsy was gone and had been for several days. And for some reason, Rodney didn't want anyone to know.

Although I occasionally do slip and have a Bitsyish moment, I draw the line at falling apart in uncertain situations. It's a waste of time and, besides, what's the point? What I did do, now, was look in the freezer to see just how much frozen bass Bitsy had been blethering on about last week. It seemed to me that the fish must have reached critical mass and were the catalyst for whatever had happened.

The freezer was empty of fish. I found frozen peas and beans, bagels and something about the size and general shape of a woodchuck that I couldn't identify but had 'Leona's: Do Not Open' in big letters on it, and a pint of chocolate chip cookie dough ice cream that I replaced regretfully. There were parcels labeled 'lasagna' and 'beef stew' and quite a few marked 'zucchini puree'. But no fish.

I decided I might as well make this a full-scale snoop and I headed for the bedroom. The bed was unmade and though I didn't look closely, I was pretty sure it was Rodney's underwear and socks lounging in the corner and not Bitsy's.

In the bathroom something struck me as odd but I couldn't at first figure out what. Then it hit me. The shower curtain was missing. Back when Bitsy was in the throws of being delighted that Rodney at last had a hobby that was getting him out of the house, she'd gone a little overboard in encouraging him. She got her hands on a catalogue from someplace called Bob's Bass Boutique and ordered a bass bedecked shower curtain. It was pretty awful, but Rodney apparently loved it. Only, now it was missing.

I sat on the edge of the tub, which wasn't very comfortable, and added things up. Bitsy absent. Fish absent. Shower curtain absent. Zero plus zero plus zero. Nothing.

I got up and went to look in her closet, hoping, I guess, to find her suitcase absent, too. Maybe she had done the most un-Bitsyish of things and taken off in some sort of snit. It seemed unlikely. Bitsy in a snit only usually makes it as far as my house. Otherwise she doesn't even go to the grocery store without a plan of attack.

Her suitcase was present and accounted for. As were most of her pairs of pointy-toed shoes all snuggled down in the shoe bag hanging on the door. There were no empty hangers. Her sock and underwear drawer appeared to be full. At this point I said something like 'oh hell'.

"Maybe she has two suitcases," Gene said that evening as we sat at my kitchen table.

"She probably has a complete matching set. But what about the hangers in the closet? And her shoes? And her underwear drawer?

"You don't know how many pairs of shoes she actually has or how full the drawer usually is and maybe she only took things that she doesn't hang up."

"Good point." Still, I gnawed my lower lip, unconvinced. "It bothers me, Gene."

"Call Rodney again."

"He's not home. He's not at his office."

"Sometimes he has late appointments."

"You're so logical." I sat quietly for awhile, only drumming my fingers annoyingly on the table a few times. "You don't maybe want to take a quick run out to the fishing shack and just take a peek?" I asked, straining to sound casual. Somehow I couldn't get rid of a picture flitting through my head of Bitsy's well-shod feet sticking out the door of the shack, the shower curtain making it's appearance as the hem of a long and rather dreadful gown.

Gene has a wonderful way of knowing what's passing through what passes for my mind. He looked at me now like I was nuts and laughed so hard he got hiccups and I had to pound him on the back. But that restored me to my wayward senses and I started to laugh, too, and didn't stop until I was sputtering.

"Oh, god, Gene. Okay. I needed that. They probably had a fight and Rodney's too embarrassed to admit Bitsy's disappeared for a few days to cool off. Wow, though. This is a departure for her in more ways than one. Go, Bitsy!" And so I chalked it all up to one more thing among many to marvel over where Bitsy is concerned.

Saturday, the day of the Big Bass Charity Tournament, Banquet and Ball, Gene set out at some unbearable hour for the lake. The plan was for him to fish his heart out along with all the other bass boffins until the official quitting time. This was set early enough in the afternoon so that everyone would be able to go home and hose off the essence of bass before the evening's gala banquet. My plan was to sleep until a bearable hour and then get up and sell a lot of books. After which we'd meet up and lend our talents to the groaning board and the dance floor. But the best laid plans and all that. Gene called me from the Marina.

"Margaret, have you talked to Barbara since you went over to Bitsy's yesterday?"

I snarled something impolite to let him know the hour wasn't bearable yet. Then, realizing that Gene isn't one to rouse an early Margaret on a whim, I pulled myself together.

"No. Why?"

"She's out here at the marina seeing Mort off. You should've heard her giving Rodney the third degree."

"Oh, poor Rodney. That'll teach him to tangle a web. What happened?"

"Not a whole lot. I was finally able to distract her and Rodney got away out onto the lake. But I bet she pops in on you sometime today."

I thanked him for the advanced warning, wished him big fish and slid from my nice warm bed into a nice warm shower. Afterwards I slid some nice hot coffee down my throat and felt ready to handle whatever came at me in the way of business or Barbara.

Business came at a steady trickle. Saturdays bring in a different set of customers from regular weekdays. There are more young families out strolling, more young professionals who've shed their suits but not their credit cards and more browsers and amiable chatterers.

Barbara came at me just as my last cup of coffee wore off. And she did it in a way that reminded me of someone. That someone, of course, being Bitsy. I thought I might have to start calling Barbara 'Babbs' to make the whole picture complete. She was looking pretty severe as she approached the counter. I finished ringing up a sale and smiled at her. Probably not convincingly.

"What can I do for you, Barbara?"

"I'm worried sick!"

"Oh, well let me show you the self-help section."

"Margaret!" Where had I heard that before? "Do you know where Bitsy is?"

"No. But don't worry, she'll turn up."

"You're not taking this seriously enough. I think something's happened to her and I think Rodney knows what and I think that friend of yours, what's his name, is in cahoots with him and I'm going to find out what's going on!"

With that she flounced out. I give her only about a six in flouncing. She could stand to take a few lessons from Bitsy in that department. Well, she obviously had her day all planned so I didn't give her any more thought. And I didn't waste any more time worrying about Bitsy. Barbara was putting enough energy into that for both of us. Besides which I had every confidence that Bitsy would reappear. Probably when I was least prepared. So I decided to enjoy whatever might be left of my Bitsy-free environment before that happened.

Barbara called me on her cell phone later in the afternoon. I rolled my eyes at her over my own phone.

"Margaret, I'm out at that fishing shed place, you know? And I've found something."

"Fish?"

"What?"

"What are you even doing out there, Barbara? And why are you calling me?"

"Well, I thought you'd at least be interested in where your sister is."

"She's not really at the shack, is she?"

"Margaret, I've found blood!"

"You're kidding. On the table outside?"

"Yes!" she squealed.

"Oh my god! Do you realize what that means, Barbara?"

"What?"

"Someone forgot to sluice it down after cleaning their damned fish again!"

"Well!" She disconnected, probably wishing she could have slammed it in my ear.

Gene swung by after his hard day on the open lake taunting fish in the dappled sunshine. He hadn't had much luck and was a little down in the mouth so I told him about Barbara's gruesome discovery of the fish-cleaning table and that cheered him up. Then I wiggled into my small black and he said I was the catch of the day as far as he was concerned. He's corny that way sometimes.

The marina has a room used for everything from rummage sales to Halloween haunted houses to wedding receptions. Tonight they were calling it a ballroom. Some of the decorations were pretty obviously leftover from the last rummage sale and/or haunted house, but the overall atmosphere was about right for a Bass Ball.

The tournament, this year, was a charity fund-raiser for the first time, benefiting the local women's shelter. It was a move applauded by many in town and resulted in more entries than they'd had in past years. There were trophies for various categories of winners and the promise of a nice fat check for the shelter.

We looked around and found Rodney when we got there, then steered toward a table that was already mostly full of people we didn't know. Gene and I had decided on the way over that we'd try to avoid Barbara and any of her pals to save Rodney, not to mention us, any further ordeals along her lines. We ate our Trout Amandine and were perfectly happy not asking Rodney where Bitsy was. He looked especially pleased with himself and perfectly happy not telling us why she wasn't there. It was a pleasant meal.

Ah, Paradise

As pleasant as a meal can get, anyway, when the conversation involves nothing but bass.

As a really great looking dessert full of chocolate and nuts and whipped cream and crystallized ginger was being served that I planned to give my undivided attention to no matter how thrilling the bass babble was getting, the Master of Ceremonies stood up and announced it was time to hand out the trophies. Rodney came as close to looking animated as I've ever seen him. He even pushed his dessert aside, so I reeled it in trusting the small black to cope.

Maybe if I did believe in second sight I would have seen what was coming. Or at least if I had divided my attention. It wasn't hard catching up, though.

Three or four names of trophy winners had already been called to general hooting and applause. I didn't recognize them and continued savoring the nuts and ginger. Then Rodney's name was announced and he shot out of his chair like a bass after a woolybugger. What happened next was like a slow motion water ballet.

Our table was toward the back of the room on the right. Rodney wended his way on a diagonal toward the center aisle. Barbara popped out of a doorway halfway up the other side of the room and made gestures in Rodney's direction that Gene later described as looking like a slip of duckweed wafting in a swiftly flowing current. You'll notice Gene has a bit of the poet about him.

A man I didn't know, galvanized by Barbara's arm waving, struck out from the left rear quadrant of the room on a path to intercept Rodney. As the two of them met up and engaged in an odd sort of two step, Bitsy, astonishingly underdressed in a pale pink sweatsuit, sailed out of a door on the right at the front of the room. She tacked toward the podium and claimed the trophy to what ended up being a standing ovation because, noticing Barbara, Rodney, and the other guy standing there, everyone else jumped to their feet, too.

Gene and I were equally agog.

"Where'd Bitsy materialize from?" he asked.

"Who's the guy with Rodney?"

We shrugged our mutual ignorance and joined the rest of the audience in the applause. I found myself clapping as much for Bitsy and the apparently successful conclusion of her departure as for Rodney and his winning largemouth.

I'm short and Bitsy's shorter so during the general clap-fest I didn't see her sail back out of the room. By the time everyone sat down, again, Rodney, Barbara, and the other man were gone, too. Gene and I shrugged again, figuring all was well. Then it was time to hand the check over to a representative for the women's shelter. Everyone clapped again. The music started up and people started dancing. Being blessed or cursed, as it may be, with only first sight and hindsight, Gene and I stayed and enjoyed ourselves, waltzing into the wee hours.

Having Bitsy for a sister, I pretty much don't even need those two feeble senses to keep track of the errors of my life. She's always happy to clue me in.

"I can't believe you didn't call the police!" blared out of the phone first thing the next morning. Temporarily stunned and still bleary-headed from the late night, I was slow in responding. "You weren't even upset that I was missing!"

"But, Bitsy," I finally managed to croak, "you weren't missing. You just disappeared for a few days."

"And what, precisely, is the difference?" Bitsy was back with a vengeance. "Barbara told you she found blood and all you did was make a joke."

"It was fish blood."

"You didn't know that. You didn't even bother to go look. At least Barbara had the decency to call her cousin the deputy."

"Is that who that guy was? He didn't arrest Rodney, did he?"

"If you'd bothered to notice what was happening last night you wouldn't have to ask that and you could've given me moral support when I went to get him out. And Rodney says you didn't even ask where I was last night!"

"Did he know?"

"No. But apparently you weren't interested enough to find that out, either."

"Bitsy, I figured you were somewhere blowing off steam."

She was silent for a minute. I pictured her gaping like a hooked fish. But probably not in admiration of my deductive abilities. More likely in annoyance that I'd found her out.

"Why don't you tell me all about it?"

"I don't know if I will." But, of course, she did. At length. I rearranged the pillow behind my head, ready for the long haul.

Following the episode of the bass bailing out of the freezer onto her foot, things had been a little strained around her house. She spent the next few days limping. Knowing Bitsy, the limp was probably more aggressive than pathetic. But by that Saturday, in an effort to restore calm, she'd set about baking for the Garden Club meeting. Baking is therapeutic for Bitsy.

"Almond biscotti and herbed bagels," she said when I asked her what she'd made. "Very time consuming, both of them, but worth it. It just makes me want to scream every time I think about it!"

I hastily pulled the phone away from my ear just in case. All was quiet. I put the phone back.

"Sounds delicious, Bitsy. Got any leftovers?"

"Why do you torture me?" she shrieked. And I got a high decibel rendition of the rest of the story.

Rodney had risen early Sunday morning and eaten some of the biscotti and bagels for breakfast. Then he'd had a brainstorm.

"He took every last bit and used it for fish bait!" The secret of Rodney's success. "He left a note saying 'Hope you don't mind, I've taken some for an experiment. I bet the bass'll go crazy.'" That's when she went crazy.

She yanked every package of frozen fish out of the freezer and tossed it all into a couple of plastic garbage bags. But the bottoms broke out because Bitsy uses cheap bags.

"Then it came to me! The shower curtain! So I yanked it down, bundled up that bass, and hit the road!"

"That's kind of what I figured, Bitsy," I said with real admiration.

"Baloney! I've never done anything like that before in my life! For all you knew Rodney killed me, rolled me up in the shower curtain, and dumped me somewhere! Did that even occur to you?"

"Well, the thought did cross my mind," I admitted, because really, I'm not at my brightest first thing in the morning.

"I knew it! I knew it! And you didn't even call the police!"

This was where I had come in. A good place for my own departure. Quietly, so as not to derail the train of her tirade, I put the phone down on the bedside table, and, without a fumble, I pulled the plug from the wall.

Settling back into my pillow, enjoying the renewed silence of the fresh morning, I closed my eyes. I could see hell to pay looming in my future, but for now, ah, paradise.

The dog in this story was inspired by two rescue dogs – ours and a neighbors – and a third dog who showed up nameless in a dream. The story was also an attempt to reassure my sisters that neither of them is Bitsy, which is something they've worried about. In No Can Do, readers learn that Bitsy can whistle. Neither of my sisters can, so I thought this would solve the problem. Did it? Sadly, no. "Now," they say, "you're just making fun of us." Ah well.

First published in Alfred Hitchcock Mystery Magazine, July/August 2001.

No Can Do

It is one of the very few bitter disappointments in my otherwise agreeable life that I can't whistle. Not a tweet. I've tried putting my lips together and they just won't blow. And I've always wanted to whistle. I'm an idly-whistle-a-tune kind of person. I can see myself whistling as I stroll down some mossy lane, or whistling to keep myself company in the lonesome hours, or just whistling as I go about my business day. But I can't and so I don't. My sister Bitsy, on the other hand, can.

Those of you who know us are probably now imagining the unkind remarks and acrid rejoinders that fly between us on the subject. Remarking and rejoining are two things we both can and often do. Hard as it may be to believe, though, not a single cross word has ever been exchanged. Really. Of course that's only because Bitsy doesn't, or at least didn't, know of my bitter affliction. And she never would have known if Rodney hadn't stolen the dog. Or, for that matter, if she hadn't then foisted the hot dog off on me.

But she's wrong about why I've been avoiding her since then. Being a receiver of stolen goods didn't particularly bother me.

And the citation for disturbing the peace was, while annoying and slightly embarrassing, hardly something to keep me down for long. After all, these things happen and I'm mature enough to accept that and move on. No, what I've been trying to avoid is the inevitable and immature scene we'll have the first time she makes use of her new found knowledge. Which she will do.

"Rodney called me yesterday," my sometimes-dear-one Gene said over a cup of coffee one morning at my sun dappled kitchen table.

"He called you what?"

"Well, I thought he called me a dog but it turns out he was asking me if I wanted a dog."

"That's not really up to you, is it? I think Old Geezer should have some say in the matter." Old Geezer is my former feline housemate who's been rooming with Gene since an unfortunate incident involving several of Bitsy's goldfish. They are now two disreputable, though decidedly charming, bachelors in one pad.

"I told Rodney three would be a crowd."

"Mm. Oh, hey, speaking of a crowd, do you want to go to the opening at the museum Sunday? It's for the watercolors on loan from the National Gallery. They've got the exhibit for two months but Jill is anxious about the opening."

He looked stricken, as though I'd just scheduled him for a double root canal.

"What's wrong? You like watercolors. You like openings. Jill needs warm bodies."

"I love all three, damn! I have to fly to Chicago tomorrow and I won't be back until Monday. That's why I came over."

"To say goodbye to my warm body?" That sidetracked him for awhile until I distracted him by pouring him another cup of coffee.

"Will you feed Geezer while I'm gone?" he asked.

"Sure."

"I'm really sorry about the opening. You could take Geezer and pass him off as me."

"I'd get tired of explaining why you were slinking off into corners and hacking up hair balls. No, I'll probably go by myself but when you get back we can go over together and have a good goggle at the pictures." We left it at that and he spent a few more minutes enjoying one of the three things he said he loves before heading for his office.

I got myself another cup of coffee and buzzed around opening the bookstore for the day. I was interviewing someone that morning, hoping to find a good part time bookseller. I only ever have two or three people working for me and they tend to stick around so I don't do this very often. It's always a bit of an adventure.

Over the past ten years I've kept a list of the questions that seem to work in an interview and those that don't. There are obvious ones like what do you like to read and can you make change? But there's always something that never occurs to me to ask someone who seems to be otherwise reasonably intelligent. Questions like do you have a short-term memory? Do you have a phobia about paper cuts? Can you spell penguin? The answers to these questions and others like them turn out to make some difference in how well a person might do as a bookseller.

Mine is a small bookstore, small enough that it and I are able to share my house without getting in each other's way or on each other's nerves much. The Internet is helping me compete in the strange new ether community that's out there somewhere. But the heart of my business is still here in this town. It belongs to the little boys who come in looking for *Redwall* books and the big sister who takes a copy of *Charlotte's Web* off the shelf and says in a hushed voice "I love this book." There's nothing like it when a customer says she shops here because we know that *Winnie the Pooh* wasn't originally set to music and we've heard of Dostoyevsky and we know things like how to pronounce Godot and that Dick Francis isn't dead.

So I was hoping that Louise, my interviewee, would be on that sort of wavelength. And I was hoping we would have a quiet morning because I really should have scheduled the interview for after hours. Louise was due at 10:00. Bitsy showed up at 9:30.

"Oh, Bitsy, is that a dog?" Good thing I wasn't interviewing myself. I sounded like an idiot.

Bitsy didn't seem to have any breath left to notice my inane question and let the dog pull her over to the counter. The dog then stood on its back legs and rested its elbows next to the cash register as though it expected a beer. It happily panted hello at me.

"Well, he's a handsome devil, Bitsy. What is he, some kind of hound? Is this what they call a black and tan?" Bitsy looked a little disheveled. I enjoyed that and told the dog he was a good boy. "It is he, isn't it Bitsy?"

"Margaret," Bitsy finally said, panting a bit herself. "Yes, it's a dog and it's male. Margaret, you've got to help me."

"Looks to me like you and Rover are doing all right on your own, Bitsy." She quelled any further flippancy with a practiced eye. "Okay," I said, restraining myself about as well as she was restraining the dog, "what's the problem? Other than there's a dog in my bookstore?"

"First, do you mind if I put him in the backyard? I'm tired of being dragged around." Apparently I'm no better at asking all the right questions in real life than I am at asking them in interviews. The question I should have asked at this point was how long do you plan to leave him in the backyard? I hate it when these things slip by me. Bitsy came back with a coffee mug in her hand and an unhappy look on her face.

"This coffee is cold."

"It's also old. What's up with the dog?"

"Oh, I am an absolute wreck!" she exclaimed. And she threw her arms out in a gesture of abandon, I assume so that I could get a good look at the wreck she'd become. The effect was lost on me, though, because I was busy grabbing the coffee mug from her before she sloshed it across the counter. She then gave a pneumatic sigh and sort of collapsed inwardly and proceeded to tell me that the dog was a stray Rodney had rescued and brought home.

"Do you think men get strange in middle age?" she asked. I opened my mouth and closed it again. It wasn't worth the aggravation to say what I wanted to. "But Margaret, what it comes right down to is I just cannot keep that dog!"

"Why not?" Here I was being disingenuous. I could tell at first pant that Bitsy and that dog weren't mixing. But sometimes it's instructive hearing Bitsy explain these things herself. The times that try her soul are the same that give me brief glimpses into the wonder that is her life.

"Let's just say that I put up with it when he vaulted over the back of the sofa and landed in my lap but the last straw was when I went into the kitchen and found myself looking at his kneecaps because he was standing on the kitchen table."

I took advantage of a sudden compulsion to dust and bent down to retrieve a dust rag from under the counter. And to wipe the smile off my face.

"So take it to the pound," I said, resurfacing.

"No! I couldn't! I mean, Margaret, have you looked him in the eyes? They can only keep dogs three or four days and then they'd have to destroy him! I couldn't."

"An ad in the newspaper?"

"I was thinking he would be a good companion for Leona." She said this very quickly and very softly.

I'd crossed the room and was redistributing the dust on the shelves in the literature section. I turned back to her now thinking I hadn't heard right. Leona is our elderly and increasingly frail cousin. Anything larger than a hamster or faster than a turtle might bowl her over. "Sorry, Bitsy, what did you say?"

"Pets are good for older people and dogs can be trained to help. You know, you've seen it on t.v."

"Are you nuts?" It was an honest question, calmly put. I was genuinely interested. "How do you picture him helping her? Will he boil the water for her tea? Fertilize her African violets? Oh, now there's a lovely image."

"Well then let me leave him here until Rodney finds a home for him."

"Oh, no, Bitsy..." I had a sinking feeling.

"You've got a fenced in backyard. You won't even have to walk him." She paused, then added "Lord knows he can't hurt anything out there if he digs around a little."

"Oh, no..."

"You like animals. He'll be a watch dog."

"Oh..."

"You took in that mangy cat."

"Cats are different, Bitsy, they can look after themselves."

"And we all know how capable that fleabag was." I could only look at her. "You owe me, Margaret." I pled with my eyes. "Gosh," she said, ignoring my eloquent baby blues. "Look at the time! I have a hair appointment at 10:00."

The door slammed shut behind her and I sank completely onto the kick stool at my feet, head in my hands, my joie de vivre dying like a dog.

"What is that noise?"

Up to this point the interview with Louise had been going well. She seemed pleasant, had retail experience, and said she liked reading biographies. I was mildly relieved to see she sported no obvious stray piercings and she was happy with the idea of weekend hours. As to the sound she'd just mentioned, I'd been hearing it, too, and couldn't quite place it.

"It sounds like the hound of the Baskervilles," she said. I gave her points for making an apt literary reference. And then I swore quietly but thoroughly under my breath.

"Excuse me, will you?" I zipped through to the kitchen. The dog was sitting outside the back door baying. What a noise. I opened the door thinking he just needed reassurance that he hadn't been abandoned. Although as far as I was concerned he had been.

"There, there, good dog. Whoa!" He threw himself into my arms and panted heavily in my face. We waltzed in the doorway for a minute and then I managed to shove him back out and close the door. He bayed. Shaking my head, I invited him into the kitchen. He panted. Swearing a little less quietly but still thoroughly I closed the door to the kitchen and returned to the interview.

"Sorry, dog sitting for my sister."

"Oh, what kind?"

"The ratty kind." She looked confused. "My sister. The dog is some kind of hound. Actually it's a stray her husband rescued."

"Oh, poor thing. What's his name?"

"Well, I guess he didn't come with one, so maybe we can give Baskerville a try and see how he likes it."

Louise liked that idea and seemed to like the idea of working in a bookstore too.

"Hope he stops baying soon!" she said, raising her voice enough so I could hear her. We agreed she should start in two weeks and we said goodbye to the accompaniment of Baskerville's dulcet tones.

For the next couple of hours I experimented with various approaches to dog shushing. That someone had mistreated this poor guy was obvious in the way he cowered at any abrupt gesture or the slightest raising of my voice. No wonder he'd cut and run when he got the chance. And looking into his eyes, I knew why Bitsy couldn't think of taking him to the pound. If I'd taken lessons from him in the soulful peeper department, maybe the two of us wouldn't now be joined at the hip. The only effective way I found to shut him up was to let him follow me everywhere.

But that doesn't necessarily work in a retail business. Not everyone coming in the door is going to be fond of dogs. And besides, I didn't really know this one. It wouldn't be a good idea to grant him free range of the place before finding out how he handled himself with strangers coming and going all day. And then there was the panting. If he wasn't making cow eyes at me he was panting. It made him look happy to be near me and apparently he was. But it also made the atmosphere humid with dog breath anywhere in his general vicinity.

I finally had to put him back out in the yard after lunch. I guiltily avoided his eyes and promised him I'd take him on a long walk after supper when I went over to Gene's to feed Geezer. He howled for the next half-hour and then the neighbors started calling. Cousin Leona, who lives next door, was first.

"Margaret, dear, did you know there is a large dog in your backyard?"

"Dog? What happened to my kangaroo?"

"Don't be silly, Margaret. What do you intend to do about it?" I explained the situation to her and expressed my sincere hope for an early resolution to the problem. She hmphed at me. I don't know if that was a specific comment on my ability to handle the situation or just a general comment on where the world was going to in its hand basket today.

I ended up repeating the conversation pretty endlessly with each and every formerly friendly neighbor. Most of them were surprisingly nice about it and agreed to be patient. Except for Mrs. Barnett who thrives on the unpleasant details and problems of her neighbors' lives. She threatened to call the police. I ignored her because that's what we all do. But when one of the neighbors called back to ask if I'd been beating the dog to make it howl so, it was just too much.

"Baskerville, here boy!" He'd taken himself off into the corner by the garage and was looking terribly forlorn and living up to his trial name. But of course not responding to it in any way. Mostly because he was making too much noise to hear me. "Baskerville, come on boy!"

"If he's a stray, how do you know his name?" Leona had tottered over to the fence and was surveying my foster dog with a pained look on her face.

"We're just trying it out." I waved my arms to attract his attention. "Hey, Baskerville! Over here!" He caught sight of my wild semaphore and cut himself off in mid bay to come bounding over. And pant.

"So what are you going to do with him now?" asked Leona.

"The two of us are going inside. He'll follow me around and breathe heavily, and I'll take a couple of aspirin."

"Well, there's a name for him," she said, turning back to her house. "Aspirin."

"Aspirin? What are you talking about?"

"Because he's a pill and also a bayer," she called over her shoulder and stumped off across her yard.

Once inside I called another pill I know.

"Margaret," Bitsy said after I'd greeted her with what I liked to think was a frosty voice, "is what's-his-name standing next to you?"

"If you're referring to all the heavy breathing, Bitsy, no, that's not Gene. That's your pal the wonder dog. He's happy to hear your voice. Why don't you come take him home?"

"Oh, sorry, no can do. Rodney's insurance banquet is tonight. He's up for Salesman of the Year again, you know." Well, that was quite an honor, I will admit. And I could picture her preening as we spoke. But if there is ever an award for Sarcastic Sister of the Year, it's mine.

"Well, that's just great. While he's been busy selling all that insurance, how much time has he actually spent looking for a new home for Aspirin?"

"I always take Tylenol, myself."

"Aspirin is your wonder dog. And he's not doing wonders for my neighborly relations or my business. Bitsy, the only time he isn't baying or howling is when he's sitting right next to me."

"Oh, I can't believe I forgot to tell you! There's a trick to that that Rodney discovered. When he howls you give a good sharp whistle, like this." I think my eyes crossed. I know she pierced my eardrum. I was still shaking my head trying to recover the hearing in that ear when she continued. I quickly put the phone to my other ear. "A good sharp whistle like that and he's quiet as a mouse. Now I have to dash. Bye!"

I looked at Aspirin and he looked at me. Maybe that was why he always seemed to be smiling. He knew my bitter secret and he knew he had me wrapped around his little paw. He followed me out to the kitchen where I grabbed the newspaper and we returned to the store, I to peruse the classifieds, he to befog my ankles with kindly meant dog breath.

Bitsy hadn't answered my question about putting an ad in the paper and I was hoping that was because Rodney had already placed one. But, no, apparently not. Maybe the number of well-bred dogs looking for homes had daunted him. Every ad in the paper was for an AKC this or an AKC that. What chance would poor old Aspirin have next to them? What did he have and the others didn't that I could capitalize on for an ad?

"You're just an old hound, aren't you, boy?" I said to him. He smiled and panted and melted my heart a little more with his Elvis eyes. And then I think he saw the light bulb go on over my head because he sighed with an extra strong gust and put his head down on my shoe for a blissful dog nap. I called the paper and placed an ad starting out "He ain't nothin' but a hound dog."

All was not chew toys and fetched blue suede slippers after that, though. We had to wait for morning and hope there would be some response to the ad. And a long afternoon, evening, and night stretched out before us. While he napped with his nose on my shoe I toyed with the idea of changing his name to Elvis. It somehow seemed too obvious, but he really did have the eyes for it. When he woke up refreshed and panting I tried it out.

"How's it going, Elvis?" I asked. He gave one sharp yelp and shot away from me as though I'd thrown scalding water in his face. It's interesting in retrospect how many books a berserk dog can tumble from the shelves of a bookstore in passing.

After he made several circuits of the place I managed to get him aimed toward the kitchen and shut the door behind him.

Some of the customers who were obliged to scale the shelves to get out of his way probably won't be darkening my doorway again. But I eventually stopped hyperventilating and he eventually calmed down. I could tell because he started baying again.

The long walk to Gene's that evening was good for all of us. Anything-But-Elvis, my neighbors' ears and me. ABE apparently wasn't holding a grudge against me for calling him Elvis and I decided he'd just been asserting his good taste in rejecting the name. He was probably more of an opera guy. He trotted along happily at the end of the leash Bitsy had left with him. We stopped occasionally to look at trees and fire hydrants and by the time we got to Gene's even I was panting. Not wanting to spring him on Geezer and provoke internecine strife, I left him tied to the railing on Gene's deck. I fed the cat and Luciano entertained Gene's neighborhood with his swelling song.

That night I tried my best to make suitable silent sleeping arrangements that didn't include a tenor sharing my pillow. My success at that can be measured by how little sleep either of us got and how swiftly Mrs. Barnett actually called the Police. And persistently. And how could I blame her? He was driving me nuts, too.

I explained the dog and his neurosis to the nice policeman who came knocking on my door. And when he came knocking again I promised to try harder. And when he came again and handed me a citation for disturbing the peace I nearly cried. He offered to take Luciano to the pound for me but I figured as long as I'd have to pay the fine anyway, I should at least get to keep the dog, and the night was already shot. So I sort of dozed sitting up on the sofa while Luciano slept on my feet.

In the morning we stumbled blearily outside to fetch the paper and exulted over the ad together. Then I called Bitsy.

"My god!" she cried. "You had the police there?"

"It wasn't my idea, Bitsy."

"Did they see the dog?"

"He suffers from separation anxiety and has bonded with my feet. So, yes, the policeman saw the dog."

"But I don't understand," she wailed. "I told you how to keep him quiet. Why didn't you whistle?"

Luciano might not know when to keep his yap shut, but I do. I didn't say anything now, partly because I didn't want to answer Bitsy's question and partly because I was surprised at the depth of her empathy, depth being the keyword. As much as I hate to sound suspicious of my own sister, I sensed an ulterior anxiety working here. So I thought a bit while she wailed on and then tried steering the conversation in a slightly different direction.

"You know he was perfectly quiet when I took him for a walk last night. Except when I tied him up outside Gene's apartment while I went in to feed Old Geezer."

"You took him for a walk? All the way across town?" She sounded pretty aghast.

"Sure. And I think it did us both some good. But I probably won't have to walk him anymore after today because the ad's in this morning's paper."

There was silence for a minute and then her voice came, as though echoing from the well of doom. "Ad?" she said. "In the paper?"

"Yeah. I figured Rodney hadn't gotten around to placing one yet. So I did."

"Unhhunhh!" she ululated. If people still have attacks of the vapors, I think that might be what she was doing now. But I could tell when she'd calmed down again because, like Luciano, she started baying.

"Margaret! You don't know what you've done!"

"I'm sure you'll tell me."

"Margaret! Rodney stole that dog!"

"What?"

"I can't believe this!" she cried. "I should have known better. You never follow simple instructions. You could have left him in your backyard, you could have whistled when he barked and no one would have known he was there! I told you Rodney would find him a home. And the police! Margaret, I just can't believe this."

I was having a little trouble with it myself. This was all my fault? I was tempted to debate that and other questions she'd raised. But I decided to stick with the basic question.

"He stole the dog?"

"Rescued."

"We're speaking in euphemisms, now, right?"

"Well, Margaret, he was being kept by this awful man who had him tied to a tree! No dog house. No shelter of any kind. He was lucky when there was water in his bowl. Not to mention food. It was abuse, Margaret!"

"He stole him?"

"Stop harping on it! It's the bravest thing Rodney's ever done." Well, and it probably was. But I didn't spend much time admiring him for it.

"So is this guy going to come looking for Oscar Meyer?"

"What are you talking about?"

"Your hot dog. Thanks to being left in the dark so that I trotted him all over town yesterday and then advertised in the paper that I've got him, not to mention his own stentorian contributions to help the situation along, can I now expect the long arm of a dog abuser to show up in my formerly peaceful and dog-free bookstore, backed up by our boys in blue?" I wiped the receiver off after spitting all that out and waited for Bitsy to say something. I was expecting whatever she said to reach my ear at a fairly high decibel so when I heard her quiet, very serious words they shook me.

"I don't know. Call Rodney."

I planned to. But first I thought maybe I'd better fortify myself with some very strong black coffee. While it was brewing and Oscar, who had located a long lost glove of mine, was busy chewing, Cousin Leona knocked on the back door. Oscar panted in her direction and went back to working on the glove.

"How's Sal this morning?" she asked, carefully lowering herself onto a kitchen chair.

"Who?" I asked.

"Sal, short for salicylic acid."

"Oh, the dog formerly known as Aspirin. Right now he has his mouth full but I'm sure we'll be hearing from him as soon as my back is turned."

"So Bitsy tells me."

"She called you? Did she also tell you…" I was all set to start spitting again but Leona cut in. She has a sharp tongue and it's always effective.

"Margaret, I really don't want to hear it all again. Why don't you call Rodney? I can handle trousers."

Now, that was an odd thing for her to say and I tried not to look alarmed. Bitsy and I have been concerned for some time about Leona's fading memory, but it never occurred to us she might just suddenly go off the deep end, or even that she was wading toward it. She can handle trousers? Whose? I poured us each a cup of coffee and sat down at the table with her, trying to look casual and unconcerned.

"Sorry, Leona, what did you say you could handle?"

"The dog. Trousers." This was actually making sense to her and maybe if I'd had more sleep and about five more cups of coffee it would have made sense to me. But wishes aren't feather beds and cappuccinos.

"Trousers?"

"Haven't you noticed? He pants a lot. Now, I will keep an eye on him. We'll be fine. He can run in the back yard and I can whistle. You call Rodney and find out what exactly is going on. Then you open your shop and stop worrying." She patted my hand dismissively.

"But…"

Her look was quelling. She put two fingers in her mouth and produced a mighty and head-shattering whistle. Trousers, glove forgotten, gazed at her in absolute awe. And I, now thoroughly awake though slightly addled, gave her a mighty hug and went to call my thieving brother-in-law.

I decided to use the phone in the bookstore so I wouldn't feel self conscious under the dampening eye of Leona. There was, after all, a chance I might want to rant a bit at Rodney. But before I picked up the phone I saw a sight for sore eyes standing at the still locked door; an anxious customer. I hate discouraging anyone so desperate for books, even at ungodly business hours. They're usually parents caught up in that age old game of "Mom, guess what I need to have for school today?"

This one was a nice looking man, mid-thirties, wearing blue jeans and a work shirt. He smiled and tipped his Braves hat to me. Probably the father of a middle schooler looking for *Lord of the Flies*. I think they're reading that too young these days. Oh well, Rodney could wait a few minutes and maybe even benefit from the reduced blood pressure resulting from an unexpected early morning sale.

I unlocked the door and the man stepped in. He stopped just inside, surveying the store. I smiled and asked him to let me know if I could help him find anything.

"I don't guess you get much business in here," he said. The slow smirk spreading across his face went a long way toward erasing his pleasant looks. What do you say to someone like that? I've never known. Thankfully they're few and far between and tend not to be interested in a dialogue, anyway. "I haven't read a book since I dropped out of school," he went on.

"Well, we've got a few in case you want to change that."

"I didn't come for a book, I came about the dog." Ah.

Trousers chose that moment to pour his soul into a particularly baleful aria. Leona's answering whistle was no more than a delicate grace note. The smirking non-reader cocked his head.

"He in through there?" He nodded toward the kitchen.

It was kind of hard to say no with Trousers being so obvious. The man followed his ears and I followed him, stepping into the kitchen just in time to hear Trousers yelp and see him back, cowering, into a corner. Leona creaked to her feet and planted herself in front of the man, fists on her hips, ready to protect her charge, looking about as fierce as a baby sparrow.

"It's all right, Cousin Leona," I said with a growing sense of misgiving, "he's come to look at Trousers." She didn't budge. I was glad.

"I don't need to look at him. That's my dog. Thought I recognized his voice. Elvis! Here boy!" I cringed and so did Trousers.

"You named him Elvis?"

"Good name for a hound dog, don'tcha think? That's why I liked your ad." Me and my bright ideas.

"He doesn't seem to like you."

"Aw, he's just shy, isn't that right Elvis? And we miss each other, don't we, boy?" He squatted down and held his hand out toward Trousers who tried to shrink further into the corner, baring his teeth and growling low in his throat. The man stood again, laughing. "Guess I'll have to go get the crate. He's a feisty one."

"You can't have him." What moronic demon took possession of my tongue to utter that?

He looked me up and down making my skin crawl. "Well, I don't see anyone else busting down the door looking for him. I'll be back this afternoon after work. Oh, and thanks for taking such good care of him."

He left, leaving the three of us frozen in the kitchen. Neither Leona or I could think of anything to say. Trousers filled the gap. He howled forlornly and we didn't have the heart to ask him to stop. Leona dropped back into a chair and Trousers came over to bury his head in her lap.

"That man can't have him," she said.

"No."

I trailed back into the bookstore to lock the door again and call Rodney.

Rodney has always been a decent kind of guy. A straight arrow. Very middle of the road. He wears sans-a-belts and drives a mid-size car. They're beige. It's beige. He's beige. What would you expect, he's an insurance salesman. He wouldn't be anyone's idea of a dognapper. There are some pastimes that just require a little more excitement than one might expect from Rodney, bungee jumping and dognapping being two that come to mind.

He has a nice phone voice, though. It conveys a lot of emotion and I believed him when he told me he was sorry for all the trouble the dog was causing. But sorry doesn't help much when a nut comes calling.

"Rodney, just how dangerous do you think this guy is?"

"Margaret, can I tell you something in confidence?" he asked.

"What do you mean?"

"I mean don't tell Bitsy."

"Oh. Okay. I guess."

"I didn't steal the dog. I paid the guy for him."

"What? Do you realize you were almost responsible for two insurance claims? Make that three, because after Leona and I both dropped dead from heart attacks, I'd have come over there and strangled you to death. Why on earth did you tell Bitsy you stole him?"

"I didn't. I just, I couldn't, well…" he hemmed and hawed and I began to see how a misunderstanding might have happened.

"What, Rodney?"

"Margaret, I saw that dog tied to that tree for months. I couldn't stand it anymore and I asked the guy if he'd let me have him. I figured he didn't really care about him. He said he'd sell him to me and when I asked how much he looked me in the eye and said a hundred bucks. I knew he didn't expect me to do anything and really, what could I do? So I looked him right back in the eye and said 'mister, you just sold a dog.' It was ridiculous, I know, but I couldn't leave the dog there and when I was trying to tell Bitsy about it I had trouble getting out the part about the hundred dollars and she jumped to a conclusion and, well, you know Bitsy."

"So why don't you want her to know the truth?"

"Are you kidding? She'd never let me forget it! A hundred dollars for that dog? And besides," now he was sounding sort of smug, "she gets an interesting glint in her eye when she looks at me these days and I kind of like it." Well, well.

"All right, your secret's safe with me. And I guess it's safe to tell this guy to go jump. But I sure hope someone else comes along wanting him. He's working out to be a very expensive dog."

"Sorry about the citation, Margaret, I'll pay it. But didn't Bitsy tell you about whistling at him?"

I decided to take a risk. "Want to swap secrets, Rodney?"

"Sure. Fair is fair." How could anyone think this Boy Scout had stolen a dog?

"I can't whistle."

"Wait'll I tell Bitsy."

"Rodney!"

He chuckled. "Sorry, couldn't help it."

"Yeah, well, Bitsy won't even try to help it if she finds out."

"I understand and I'm real sorry for your disability, Margaret. But what are you going to do about the barking?"

"Leona's volunteered to be my surrogate whistler. Now, I'm counting on thousands of people calling and begging for a chance to adopt this extremely valuable animal, so goodbye."

After hanging up on my pseudo-larcenous brother-in-law I went to reassure Leona and Trousers. Trousers was already back to panting happily. Leona looked like she was deep in thought. Or maybe she was taking five. Sometimes it's hard to tell. I corralled another cup of coffee, hung out my 'open' sign and made what I hoped would be a better start on my business day.

Customers flowed in and out throughout the morning. The phone rang from time to time, mostly people looking for books, which is good because, after all, that is my business. Every once in awhile I heard Trousers begin a song followed by a sharp whistle and then the breathy silence of a happy dog panting. I don't know how Leona spent her time between whistles, maybe ripping recipes she liked out of my cookbooks. If she did, I'd probably never notice.

Only two people called about the ad. One of those hung up, disappointed that Trousers wasn't an AKC blue tick hound. So was I if it meant no one else wanted him. The other was a woman who, having just moved out in the country, wanted a dog for her children. She said they would come see him after school. I hoped school got out before work.

Around 2:30 Leona and Trousers both nodded off for the afternoon. I was working on a sales report at the counter, tempted to pull the report over me like a blanket and take a little snooze myself. But naptime never comes for the weary bookseller. I was zoning out to facts and figures and a fugue on the classical station when the bell over the door jangled, jerking me back to full consciousness.

A little boy, about eight, hopped through the door, followed closely by a slightly older boy and girl, a gangly teenager and a woman carrying a little thumbsucker.

"Look, Mommy! It's books *and* dogs!" piped the first one through the door. The other children, eyes bright with book lust, immediately dispersed to explore the shelves. The mother came up to the counter, smiling.

"What an interesting business you have," she said, "beagles and books."

"Foxhounds and folios."

"Shih tzus and short stories," she said, laughing.

I felt so much better. "I should tell you that I really don't know much about this dog. My brother-in-law liberated him from a bad situation. He likes to yell but stops if you whistle. He seems pretty calm unless you mention a certain name." I leaned across the counter and motioned for her to do the same. "He hates the name Elvis," I whispered. I straightened back up and resumed my normal tone of voice. "And he pants a lot. Would you like to meet him?"

I brought Trousers out on his leash. The children gathered in a semi-circle around him. He sat, panting happily, looking at each of them in turn.

"What's his name?"

"Today we've been calling him Trousers. But he probably wouldn't mind if you called him something else."

"Hi Trousers!"

"Trousers, you wanna come live at our house?"

The teenager took the leash and led Trousers to their old station wagon. The kids piled in the back and Trousers piled in with them.

"Thanks, I think he'll fit right in," the woman said, rearranging her armful of child to shake my hand. She smiled and the child now on her hip took the thumb out of its mouth and panted in agreement. "I'm sure we'll be back for books soon."

Leona was standing behind me when I turned around from waving after them.

"Hmph. What'll you tell that wretch Rodney stole the dog from when he comes back?"

I'm a woman of my word so I'd only told Leona that we needn't worry too much because Rodney had something on the guy that he couldn't discuss, not that he hadn't actually stolen Trousers. But that still left the question of what to say when the guy came back.

"I guess I'll bark up that tree when I get to it, Leona. Thanks for being my whistler by proxy. I couldn't have made it through another day without you." Leona was making an odd face at me and I wondered if maybe the whole thing had been too much for her. "Are you all right?" I asked. "Did all that pinch whistling wear you out?" By now she was making gurgling noises, too, as though she was strangling. I was about to leap forward and perform a Heimlich on her when she gave me a disgusted look and rolled her eyes.

"Hello, Bitsy dear," she said.

I cringed, much the way Trousers did when his former owner said "Elvis." I turned around to find Bitsy with an evil grin on her face and a glint in her eye. The glint Rodney so admired must be a different one because this one didn't thrill me. But it did tell me how long she'd been standing there. Someday I should put a bell on my kitchen door, too. I braced myself for an onslaught of ridicule, but Cousin Leona stepped between us.

"Girls! This is no time for your nonsense." We immediately regressed to being ten and twelve years old. We probably would have hopped to it if she'd told us to blow our noses and tie our shoes. She tends to be more practical than that, though. "Margaret, tell Bitsy about the dog and what's been going on. The wretch might show up any minute."

"Yes, ma'am." So I filled Bitsy in on the details of our encounter with the dreadful dog-abuser, further reinforcing her cockeyed reverence for her petty-thieving husband. And she was happy that Trousers ended up with such a nice family.

"But Margaret! What are you going to say to the man?"

"I don't know, Bitsy. I'm hoping for divine inspiration."

At that, with the typical good timing of the gods who get their kicks out of playing with our little lives, the bell over the front door jangled and our man walked in. It was probably just due to a change in the weather, but he brought a chill wind in with him. It seemed to please him that there were now three of us to give him an audience. He leaned lazily against the door, his smirk drifting easily into place.

"Where's Elvis?" he asked.

We looked at each other and the answer to that question sprang fully blown into our heads. We turned to him, as one, and said, "Elvis has left the building."

It might not exactly have been divine inspiration, but it certainly wasn't something any of us ever expected to have the opportunity to say. And it worked. He grumbled some but as I escorted him outside I let him know that I knew he didn't have a cloven hoof to stand on. He shrugged, spit on the ground and left.

Leona tottered on home after that. Bitsy stuck around and gave me a hand closing up shop for the day.

"Margaret?" she asked in an uncharacteristically subdued voice.

"Hmm?"

"I am sorry about springing the dog on you like that."

"So long as Rodney doesn't make a habit of stealing dogs."

"How about I take you out to dinner one night next week to make up for it? To the Tea Kettle."

I glanced at her quickly, not liking the way this conversation was going all of a sudden.

"And afterwards, we could go see the watercolors at the museum. I hear they have some by Wyeth and Turner. And Whistler."

"Sorry, Bitsy." I hustled her to the door. The glint in her eye was back and glowing. I pushed her out the door and locked it behind her, calling through it as I turned the sign to 'closed,' "Thanks anyway! No can do!" I left her standing there with that evil grin on her face and I've been avoiding her ever since.

A story of old books, volunteering, and strudel. It Takes Two grew from an experience I had volunteering for the annual fundraiser at my children's school. Afterwards, I was thanked for donating my "two Ts." I had to ask what that meant, and when I heard, I knew it was something Bitsy would say.

First published in Alfred Hitchcock Mystery Magazine, February 2002.

It Takes Two

My sister Bitsy called the other morning and asked me over for a cup of tea and a piece of strudel. Homemade strudel, hot from the oven. If I held the receiver out you could smell the apple and cinnamon and mouthwatering, flaky pastry over the phone. It was a nice invitation, very warm and sisterly. So tempting. Which just goes to show what a sad sack I am because it only made me suspicious. I can't help it. It's my nature. As our late mother used to say, it takes two to tangle, and the two she had in mind are Bitsy and me.

Not that we always tangle. Our relationship can't be characterized that simply. It's more like we're involved in some lifelong dance. We glide along nicely for awhile and then we hit a dip and pose dramatically at opposite ends of our sibling bond, often exchanging words not generally associated with dancing. But we always get swept up by the music again and renew the uneasy grace in our lives. If that sounds something like the tango, well, that also takes two. And it doesn't look as though either one of us is bowing out anytime soon.

Bitsy's latest passion, that which had me feeling leery of her tempting invitation, has had her grubbing around the family roots. The genealogy bug bit her and she's been working at spreading the infection. She's been sifting through papers and records and writing letters and emailing far and wide. What she's ended up with is an inflated vision of our family and the dream of someday publishing a little book detailing our illustrious lineage. Which she will expect me to sell in my bookstore. I dread the day. Not that we haven't had our flashier moments and some respectable accomplishments. But ancestor hunting has never thrilled me. And books like that tend to petrify on my shelves.

So I was tentative on the phone, wondering what might lie behind this overture.

"Margaret," she finally said, sounding exasperated. "Why are you making such a production out of this? It's tea. It's strudel. Just come over and have some."

I hung up, admiring her unusual succinctness. Was this a new leaf she'd turned over whilst investigating the family tree? The only way to find out, I decided, was to trot around to her house, something my taste buds and tummy had been begging me to do all along. I could always gallop back home again if it turned out she had a hidden agenda.

"Now this is cozy, Margaret," she said half an hour later as we sat at her kitchen table. "We should do this more often. We so rarely spend time like this together, just the two of us."

"You forgot our friend the strudel," I said, helping myself to another slice. "That makes three of us. Mmmm. You really are a great cook." See, I can be swell, too. Bitsy managed to roll her eyes and preen at the same time, something only a professional like her should try.

While she poured more tea, into teacups that actually matched the saucers and the teapot, I looked around her kitchen, marveling. Imagine not only taking the time to bake fresh strudel, but ending up with a spotless kitchen to boot, and nerves steady enough to calmly serve tea. I leaned back and let her happy prattle waft over me with the aromatic steam from my teacup.

"...so I joined the Historical Society."

I shook myself from my strudel stupor. "The Historical Society? What, are you the youngest living member?"

"Margaret." She looked pained. "They are a lovely group of people."

"Sorry, Bitsy, I know they are. Some of my very best customers are members of the Historical Society. It's just that I'd hate to see you dying your hair blue prematurely. So what's new at the Historical Society?"

"Well, this is something that might interest you." Uh oh. "Have you ever seen their little library and archives?"

"No," I said cautiously.

"They have some fascinating things. For instance, there is this one book, very rare I understand, *The Thrilling Adventures of Grenoble Grundy, Union Spy.*"

"I've read it." Bitsy raised her eyebrows. Point for my team. "I found a copy of it for Good Old Melva about eight years ago and she let me read it before she bought it." One eyebrow was now lower than the other and she was giving me the fish eye. "It was definitely thrilling," I offered. Her mouth got tiny. I shrugged. "It's what I do, Bitsy. I find ways for books and the people who love them to get together. Kind of like a dating service."

"I'm aware of what you do, Margaret. What surprises me is the casual way you refer to Miss Melva Jenkins."

"Good Old Melva? She and I are pals from way back. I only know her through the store but we've done each other a lot of good over the years. Why, is she a revered goddess of the Historical Society?"

"She's dead."

"What?"

"I guess you're not the good friends you thought you were if you didn't know that, Margaret. She died two months ago."

There was suddenly a small rent in my universe. I sat back in my chair and didn't care that my mouth was hanging open unbecomingly. Melva had slipped away without my noticing.

"Oh, Bitsy, that's so sad. I really liked her."

"Don't you read the obituaries?"

"No."

"And you accuse me of hiding from reality."

"There's a difference between being realistic and running after the morbid details."

We exchanged looks through narrow slits but I wavered first, not having the heart just now for a good tangle. Instead I sighed.

"Well, I'm sorry she's gone, too, Margaret. But I'm glad you knew her and liked her. Now I don't feel so bad asking you what I was going to."

Here it came. I knew the tea and strudel had to be spiked with an ulterior motive. What an absolutely ripping day this was turning out to be. "What?"

"Don't sound so negative, Margaret. Miss Melva Jenkins left her collection of local history books and various papers to the Historical Society and I volunteered to inventory them. We'd like an appraisal of the books for our records, as well, and I thought you might be interested in donating your two 't's to the project.

"My what?"

"Your time and talent. What do you think?"

Despite Bitsy's two 'c's (cloying cuteness), the idea was actually appealing. Good Old Melva had bought some great old books from me and I'd always hoped she'd invite me over to drool through her private library someday. Now she was gone and I'd gotten my wish. Thanks to Bitsy. Who'd've figured? So I thanked her for the tea and the strudel and I thanked her for putting me in touch with Melva one more time and the two of us made arrangements to meet at the Historical Society Sunday afternoon to start going through boxes of books.

Bitsy's car was already parked out front when I arrived at the house the Historical Society calls home. It's a nice example of a craftsman style bungalow on the opposite end of Main Street from my bookstore. The porch and foundation are made of local river rocks. Around the turn of the century there was a guy who made his living using the smoothed and rounded knobs in everything he built. His legacy is visible around town and here and there out in the county. These days people either hate the somewhat eccentric buildings or love them. I love them and was glad the Historical Society did, too.

"Hello!" I called, stepping in the front door. I heard Bitsy's answering trill coming from somewhere upstairs. Everything else was quiet. On the wall heading up the stairs was a series of framed photographs featuring members of the Historical Society down through the years. I looked at each picture as I slowly climbed and saw the members growing older before my eyes. Good Old Melva first appeared in the 1964 photo, looking about 50. I did a fast forward through her life the rest of the way up.

"It's nice to know some things never change," I said to Bitsy. She was standing at the top of the stairs with her hands on her hips.

"Like you being late?"

"You might call it late, Bitsy. I like to think of it as being reliable. I'm reliably behind schedule. No, I was talking about Good Old Melva in these pictures. I thought dressing like Queen Elizabeth was just a costume she'd adopted for her role as a little old lady."

"Margaret!"

"But it turns out she'd always dressed like that. She looked like Julia Child and dressed like Queen Elizabeth. What a great combination. Did you ever meet her?"

"No, I wish I had."

"You would have liked her. She was one of the good ones. I think I'd be happy if I knew I'd grow up to be Good Old Melva."

"If you ever grow up."

"Where are the books?"

"In here." She led the way into a back bedroom now being used as the library and archives. The walls were lined with shelves and an old library table took up the middle of the room. A dozen or so sturdy liquor boxes were stacked in a corner, 'HISTORICAL SOCIETY BOOKS' scrawled across each in black magic marker. A familiar tingle danced down my spine when I saw them and I couldn't help grinning. It's like Christmas morning every time. The promise of wonderful books lay before me. I think my fingers were wriggling in anticipation. Let me at them.

"What's your plan of action, Bitsy?"

"Don't you have one?"

"Of course I do. A bookseller is always prepared." I opened one of the boxes and took a whiff. Oh thank you, Melva, for not letting your books get musty. "Okay, how about we take them out of the boxes and roughly arrange them according to category. Paperbacks in one place, magazines and journals in another, anything that looks like family papers in another and the hardbacks in another. We can refine the categories as we go if we need to."

"Why are your cheeks all pink?"

"Don't you feel it? Don't you hear them calling? It's the books, Bitsy. They want me."

"Oh brother. Okay, let's get started."

We spent the next couple of hours sorting things into their respective piles. We could have moved faster but at times like this and with books the quality of Melva's, it's impossible not to stop and ogle a bit at each one. And Good Old Melva had some real treasures. She actually had a first edition of *Godsey's Annals*, incredibly hard to come by and very much sought after. I sat and stroked its cover until Bitsy began to look uncomfortable. She also had something I'd never even heard a whisper of. It was a limited edition, small press issue of an epic poem written for the state's centennial celebration in 1896, bound in green silk. I was completely charmed.

"Wow," Bitsy said when the last box was finally empty. She wiped the back of her hand across her forehead and pushed the hair out of her eyes. "There is some amazing stuff here!"

"Yeah, Melva was a marvel."

"She must have been." She was sitting next to the last box she'd emptied and now she shoved it out of the way and leaned back against the wall. "Tell me about her."

"Well, I told you I only knew her through the store, but it's amazing what you can learn about a person through their books."

"Like what?"

"She had class, Bitsy, real class. From her Julia child stature to her Queen Elizabeth clothes to her voice, which always made me think of Eudora Welty for some reason. But a thread of irreverence ran through everything she said and did and I don't quite picture Eudora Welty using some of Melva's vocabulary."

"What do you mean?"

"She swore like a sailor."

"Oh come on!"

"It's not only the truth, it's the goddamned truth."

"Margaret!"

"That's a direct quote from Miss Melva Jenkins. She was very funny, Bitsy."

"Well, I can see why you liked her," she said with a sniff.

"She was Good Old Melva, Bitsy. One of the best." I stopped and looked around at the piles.

"What's the matter? Disappointed there isn't more?"

"Hm? Oh, no, I was just wondering." Something was bothering me but I didn't know quite what. Of course I'd love it if there were a dozen more boxes like these to go through. I'd feel as though I'd died and gone to heaven along with Good Old Melva. But it was *something* about more books. And then I knew. "Bitsy, did Melva give all her local history stuff to the Society? Did she leave any of it to her niece or nephew?"

"As far as I know everything came to us. Why?"

"A couple of things are missing."

"What do you mean? How can you possibly know that?"

"One is the copy of *Grenoble Grundy* I sold her. It's not here. And the other is something I never saw but she told me about. It was a diary. I think it was her father's."

"Well, there's that copy of *The Thrilling Adventures of Grenoble Grundy* already here. Maybe that was hers. Maybe she gave it before she died."

"Where is it?"

She made a face but got up and scanned the shelves.

"Here. Happy?"

I took it from her and looked it over, leafing through the pages and checking the spine and endpapers. "Not Melva's copy."

"Oh, for heaven's sake. How do you know? You said you got it for her years ago."

I raised my eyebrows at her. "Eight years ago in February. Her copy didn't have any foxing and, although her copy could have gained some foxing in that time, none of her other books have suffered that way. And her copy had an inscription on the title page." She looked skeptical. "Trust me, Bitsy, this is the kind of information I clutter my brain with so that I don't have room for other things like what size bag my vacuum cleaner takes."

"That's very impressive Margaret." Somehow I didn't think she really thought so. "She probably did just give the *Grundy* and the diary to her niece or somebody."

"Or, maybe somebody bumped her off for them."

"Oh, right."

"Maybe someone stalked Good Old Melva and tipped her down the staircase. Do you know how she died? Did anyone test for arsenic?"

"I think you are being extremely tasteless." We both jumped. An elderly woman stood in the doorway. I didn't recognize her but by the way Bitsy sort of cringed, I figured she did.

"Mrs. Martin," Bitsy said, standing up straighter and using her dazzling smile to good effect. "We didn't hear you come in. We've just been going through Good Old, I mean Miss Melva Jenkins' books…"

"So I heard. I don't believe I know you." She directed this at me. Bitsy was kind enough, or cowed enough, to make the introductions.

"This is my sister, Margaret Welch. She's going to do the appraisal for us. Margaret, this is Mrs. Alice Martin, the president of the Historical Society."

"It's nice to meet you, Mrs. Martin. Your library here is very impressive and Melva's books are a wonderful addition." I thought I sounded nice but all Mrs. Martin said was "Hmph." I've been hmphed at by little old ladies before but none of them were able to give it quite the spin that Mrs. Martin did. Then she turned on her heel and we heard her huff her way down the stairs.

Bitsy and I looked at each other, Bitsy looking properly chagrined. I just wondered how long Mrs. Martin had been standing there before saying something. Hadn't her mother ever told her it was impolite to listen in on other people's conversations?

"Well, I'll tell you one thing, Bitsy," I said, hoping to cheer her up, "Good Old Melva was never one to say "hmph" at anyone."

"Oh, stop with the Good Old Melva! I am mortified! I'll probably be the only person ever thrown out of the Historical Society."

I couldn't imagine why anyone would toss her out of the Hysterical Society just because I'd been making uncalled-for jokes about Melva's death. But Bitsy often thinks she's the only person ever involved in the daily crises that make up our lives. And who knows, maybe the members would rise up as one to banish her. I didn't really think they'd have the energy to spare for that kind of thing, though. They tend to expend whatever spunk they can muster squabbling over things like which historic paint chip palette to use for re-painting the old inn.

It was getting late and the whole job of inventorying the books and giving any kind of ballpark estimate of their value was going to take a few more sessions. Bitsy half-heartedly picked up her legal pad to get started and then put it down again. It was her idea that we should come back later in the week when maybe St. Alice wouldn't be lurking. She said she'd call me some evening when the coast was clear. So we adjourned to her house for leftover strudel. That was my idea.

A funny thing about Bitsy is that she really does care what people think of her. She was genuinely worried, for instance, about Alice Martin's opinion. And although Bitsy is sometimes a little heavy-handed when it comes to laying blame, if she wanted to consider the incident in the library as being all my fault, I decided I couldn't be anything other than gracious in accepting it. It wasn't she, after all, who had run on and on about missing books and the murderous ways they might have disappeared.

So, as well as being uncharacteristically gracious, I thought I'd be generous, too. I decided to do something for Bitsy and the Historical Society to make up for joking about one of their dearly departed own. Melva's niece, Christy Orebank, had been a few years ahead of us in school. I vaguely remembered her but not enough to remember either liking or disliking her. After a little telephone work, I tracked her down to Knoxville.

"Margaret Welch? Are you the one whose nose got so sunburned every summer that we called you Rudolph?"

"Oh, yeah, right. Thanks for reminding me."

"Kids are awful, aren't they?"

"And then they grow up and become loan officers and surgeons." I explained to her how I knew her aunt and why I was calling now.

"Wow, all that old stuff? No, I've never been interested in any of it and I doubt Bill ever was, either. Aunt Melva would've known better than to leave any of it to us. No, she was pretty good to us in her will, but it was always understood that the books and family papers and everything would go to the Historical Society. But I remember the diary." She laughed, sounding a little like a younger version of Good Old Melva.

"There was some story about that diary that always made my mother turn red and Aunt Melva giggle. I don't know what it was. They always said they'd tell us about it when we were old enough. I guess by the time we got old enough we'd lost interest."

We said a few things along the lines of how isn't that the way things always go. Then I thanked her and she asked after my nose again and I managed to say goodbye without sounding too peeved.

She called back about twenty minutes later.

"Rudy?" I almost hung up. "I got to thinking about that diary and I remembered that one of the kids borrowed it for a history project."

"So you do have it?" I asked.

"No, Aunt Melva only let her have it on pain of death if she didn't return it."

"Well, rats." So why'd she bother to call me back?

"But she transcribed it. Do you think the Historical Society would like a copy of the transcription?"

"To quote your aunt, not only yes, but hell yes."

"That was Aunt Melva, all right," she laughed. "I'll put it in the mail for you tomorrow."

I thanked her again and this time didn't have any trouble sounding sincere.

The transcription arrived a few days later. Bitsy hadn't called me in the meantime to schedule any furtive book appraising. Maybe I was already too late and she'd been booted out of the society. She might be in seclusion, keeping her shame hidden behind drawn shades. I didn't really think that was the case, though, because I would have been the first to hear about it. Loudly and at great length.

I thought about calling her, now, and telling her the good news about the copy of the diary. But it was a slow afternoon in the bookstore and, even though I tried burying it under some bills, I finally couldn't resist that thick brown envelope. I retrieved it without disturbing the bills and settled myself comfortably on the stool behind the counter to read.

Melva's father must have had the dominant genes in that family. It was pretty obvious where her charm, irreverence, vocabulary and name had come from. Good Old Melvin Jenkins, Jr., was a character, even as a teenager. His father had given him the diary for his fifteenth birthday in 1899 and he'd written in it off and on until he'd gone off to college somewhere in the Midwest.

I wished I could hold the real thing in my hands. I wished Melva's great niece had been a better typist. But I enjoyed my afternoon with Melvin, aged 15 through 18. Especially age 17 through 18. He developed an interest in astronomy about then and his father gave him a telescope for his seventeenth birthday. Most of his diary entries after that described the moon and the stars and the other heavenly bodies he spent hours gazing upon. He apparently spent hours and hours gazing. And the descriptions were pretty detailed. No wonder Melva had giggled and Christy's mother turned red.

My elderly cousin, Leona, stopped in while I was in the middle of a particularly colorful passage.

"Leering doesn't become you, Margaret," she said by way of greeting.

I composed myself and asked how she was feeling. She's not quite as old as Melva was, but she is getting frail. She said she was feeling fine, which would have been her answer even if I'd caught her taking her last breath. Then I thought of something else to ask her.

"Cousin Leona, do you know anyone named Agnes Mae Pritchard?"

"Agnes Pritchard Kelley, that would be. She married the banker, Arthur Kelley. She was quite a famous beauty in her day, or so my mother used to say. I haven't heard her name in years. Why?"

"I've been reading an old diary. Melvin Jenkins'."

"Melva Jenkins' father? Good heavens, I remember him." I don't recall ever seeing Cousin Leona blush before. Obviously Melvin's eye for the ladies hadn't dimmed in middle age. Leona didn't stay for her usual cup of tea.

Bitsy called as I was closing up shop for the day.

"Is the coast clear?" I whispered.

"Yes, Margaret. And try to control yourself this time."

"Sorry, Bitsy. I'll see you there. Oh, and I have something for you."

"What?"

"Don't sound so suspicious. You'll like it. Trust me."

"Yeah, right."

Now why was she being like that?

We met that evening to perform our clandestine inventory and ended up not getting a lot of work done after all. For one thing, Bitsy was delighted with the transcription and I spent most of our time entertaining her by reading aloud some of the better bits. We had quite a lot of fun and I began to see this doing-things-together idea of hers in a better light.

"What a hoot!" she said when I finally put the diary aside. "And speaking of hoots, wouldn't you just give anything to know who Agnes Mae Pritchard was?"

"According to Leona she married Arthur Kelley. She was Agnes Pritchard Kelley." Bitsy's jaw dropped. "What?" I asked.

"Oh my god. Margaret. I know where the diary is."

"Where? Did the ghost of Agnes Mae bump off Good Old Melva so she could get her hands on it?"

"You are tiresomely tasteless," came a voice from the doorway.

"My two t's," I said.

"Margaret!" Bitsy hissed, turning toward the door.

And there was the other reason we didn't end up getting much work done that night.

"Mrs. Martin, how nice to see you again. Why don't you come in and sit down." Bitsy has a knack for issuing that kind of invitation. They don't come with question marks and, even though she's short and not very prepossessing, the message gets through. It might have something to do with the steely look she gets in her eye. I know it makes me jumpy. It had that effect on Mrs. Martin, too.

"And just where did you get a copy of that, that..." She tried to bluster but Bitsy held her ground.

"The diary, Mrs. Martin?"

"Filth, is more like it." Bitsy quelled any further comment by moving her left eyebrow a fraction of an inch.

"Bitsy," I said quietly, not wanting to distract her but hoping for a little enlightenment, "what's going on?"

"Margaret, let me introduce you to Alice Kelley Martin."

I managed to keep my jaw from dropping, but couldn't do anything about the smile playing around my lips. "Oh," I said. "Very good, Bitsy." And then I let the smile get completely away from me. "Mrs. Martin, I think we'd like to hear about your two 'a's."

"My what?"

"And your two 'p's. Your actionable appropriation and petty pilfering. Why did you do it?"

"Because of the scandal!"

"The scandal of a beautiful girl being described in execrable poetry by a randy 17 year old?"

"I'll be a laughing stock if this gets out!"

"I think there's more scandal in stealing the diary," Bitsy said.

"You were laughing."

"But not at you, Mrs. Martin. Not at Agnes Mae."

"At what, then?"

We looked at each other, wondering.

"At the seventeen year old in all of us," I finally said. "It's a ridiculous age but not a scandalous one. Don't you think, Mrs. Martin, that if Miss Melva Jenkins was comfortable sharing her father's diary with the Historical Society, that you should honor her wish?"

"Melva Jenkins was an old bat!" Alice Martin said and stormed out.

"Those two never got along," Bitsy said shaking her head.

"So she had the *Grenoble Grundy*, too. Mm, mm, mm. What a piece of work is Mrs. Alice Martin." Bitsy and I were sitting at the library table in the Historical Society several evenings later, surrounded by Good Old Melva's newly inventoried books. I was holding Melvin's diary and petting it as though it were a cat. It's an odd compulsion but some books just affect me that way. I stopped when I realized Bitsy was looking at me.

"She's an odd duck, all right," she said, and I wasn't entirely sure she was talking about Alice Martin. "She had a few other books that were duplicates from our collection. She returned those, too."

"How uncommonly good of her. So I guess there'll be a new president soon?"

"Oh, no."

"No? Why not?"

"Because of the scandal, Margaret. Can you imagine if word got out that the president of the society was helping herself to whatever took her fancy?"

"And what if something else catches her eye?"

"I told her I'd have my eye on her." Well that would certainly keep her in line if anything could. "So, Margaret," Bitsy said then, turning that eye on me, "now that we've finished this project, why don't we start something else?"

I was feeling pretty mellow and magnanimous. We'd had some fun together. "What did you have in mind, Bitsy?" I asked.

"The family history. Why don't we write it together? It would be such fun and with the two of us working on it we could…"

But I was already on my way out the door. I saluted Good Old Melva as I flew down the stairs, Bitsy's single echoing 'm' in my ears.

"Margaret!"

Zoo doo, eccentric customers, and rare books – these are all details from my former life as a bookseller. In Fandango by Flashlight, I took those details for a spin on the dance floor and turned them into something that never happened to me.

First published in Alfred Hitchcock Mystery Magazine, December 2005.

Fandango by Flashlight

"What in heaven's name was he doing here?" Bitsy, my one and only sister, knows how to make an entrance. She snapped the door shut, she on the inside, the object of her scorn now ambling off down the street. "I mean, really Margaret, Ed Tidwell of all people."

"Ed's all right," I said.

"He needs to be fumigated."

She looked around my bookstore with narrowed eyes, calculating my own fumigation needs. Even on its worst days, my place doesn't deserve to be lumped in with Ed Tidwell and his eccentric hygiene. But I've been on an extreme cleaning kick lately, so I let the books standing at attention on their dust free shelves and the glowing floors testify for themselves. Bitsy had to settle for glaring at me, instead. I tucked stray hair behind my ear.

"He has some books he wants me to look at," I said and couldn't help smiling.

"And you actually think Ed has anything that can possibly be worth looking at?"

"Can't help it, Bitsy. I have to look."

"My sister the biblioholic. Trust me, anything Ed touches is likely to turn into something best described as euw."

"Speaking of euw," I said, going for distraction as a way of muting further unpleasant observations about my customers rather than the roll of duct tape my fingers were itching to apply, "you know that Zoo Doo elephant Leona gave me for the front garden? It's gone."

She looked out the window. As a member of the Garden Club, it tries Bitsy's soul to acknowledge the meager patch I call a garden. She turned back to me with a mixture of patience and condescension playing a game of tag across her face. "Zoo Doo sculptures are supposed to disappear, Margaret. That's the whole point of making them out of compressed dung. The sculptures are naturally time-released fertilizer."

"But Leona only gave it to me two days ago."

"Oh. Well, there have been a number of letters to the editor recently about flower arrangements at the cemetery disappearing. Supposedly they've blown away."

Mission accomplished. I had no idea what connection she saw between wind tossed flowers at the cemetery and my Zoo Doo elephant, but at least she was no longer maligning my customers front, center, and in full voice. I try to keep my sister's opinions and my business separate, though it isn't always easy.

But, to be honest, I did agree with her about the dim chance of Ed Tidwell having any books worth looking at. Ed says he retired a few years back. By retired, he means that he quit showing up at the garage where he worked only haphazardly to begin with. He also quit cutting his hair or shaving or bathing regularly. He keeps himself together doing odd jobs around town. Two things I've learned over the years in the book business, though; you never know what you'll find in the most unlikely places, and never judge a customer by his or her cover.

And I like Ed. Mostly if I'm upwind of him, but he's one of the world's gentle souls.

"Blown away, you say? Imagine that. So, Bitsy, what can I do for you?" My sister might be opinionated, what some people prefer to call rude and overbearing, but at least she buys and reads books.

"Actually, you must be rubbing off on me. I couldn't help myself and I had to come visit our little book." The little book she referred to might break her toe, were I to drop a copy on it. It's *A Pictorial History of Stonewall*, a volume long out of print and recently back in print thanks to the Stonewall Historical Society. When Bitsy isn't gardening, she's busy being historical.

"They did a nice job on it," I said.

"Didn't they?" she gushed. She was stroking one of the burgundy covers as she might a cat. I really must be rubbing off on her. "So, come on, tell me, how many have you sold?"

"You're looking at what's left."

"You've sold all but five?"

"Six."

We looked at the stack of books, which refused, no matter how hard I stared at it, to be more than five.

"I know where the other one's gone," Bitsy said, looking pleased. "Three guesses. And they all end in euw."

"Ed didn't take it."

"Of course he took it. Think about it, Margaret. Since when does Ed Tidwell read, much less collect books, anyway? Where do you think he got the one's he wants you to fence for him?"

"He's selling them for someone who's moving."

"Hah! And if you believe that you're a fool."

"Bitsy, he just dances to a different fiddler."

"So tell me who else took it. Who else has even been in the store this morning?" She made a show of peering around at the general lack of customers. "Face it, Margaret. And I bet you something else, too. Ed's the one who took your Zoo Doo. He certainly smells like it."

I teetered at the brink of a satisfying response. But the bell over the door had jingled half way through Bitsy's remarks and it is true that there are pleasures best not mixed with business. I pulled myself together, ignored Bitsy, and smiled at Nilda, a good and frequent customer. She waved and headed for the other room. I turned back to Bitsy.

"Have fun sniffing out any treasures amongst Ed's books, Margaret. Hope you don't catch anything if you get too close."

I almost heaved a copy of the pictorial history at her, but she was already sailing out the door. I've got a good arm and could probably still have winged her, but Nilda was back with a stack of paperbacks. Being the slave to customer service that I am, I settled for a discreetly belligerent sigh.

"That was quick, Nilda," I said. "Oh, no, Hon, I brought these in for trade credit. I didn't want to interrupt you when I came in and saw you with your customer, and if you don't mind my saying so, that woman had a bee up her nose. If I'd been you, I'd have thrown something at her."

I laughed. "I should hire you as the bookstore bouncer, Nilda."

"Why, does she bother you often?"

"About every day of my life."

Nilda looked nonplused.

"That was my sister." I explained.

"Oh, well." A flip of her wrist dismissed Bitsy. "No need to tell me how that goes, Hon, I've got six of them myself. You get the seven of us together plus the five brothers and there's no telling what we're likely to stir up, I tell you what. Now, I'll get out of your hair while you figure up my credit. I'll be back there in the cookbooks."

Nilda brings me nice books. Their spines aren't broken and they don't smell of cigarette smoke or anything else they shouldn't. She's also happy to take trade credit for them to spend in the store on more books to feed her own habit. She's only been in town a few months, but ours has become a mutually beneficial relationship.

The door jingled again and my elderly cousin, Leona, tottered in. A shot of bookstore gossip is part of her morning routine. She pauses outside to deadhead the flowers I neglect for her benefit, then fusses her way inside to find out if I've heard anything new. Or to set me straight if I get it wrong.

"Margaret, dear, the cosmos are looking much perkier this morning. That Zoo Doo is a remarkable product. I wonder if they use one hundred percent elephant dung or if they mix in other species? Gazelle, for instance. And would that be an improvement? Or do they even know? Perhaps I'll offer to do a controlled study for them. How are you dear?"

"Probably not as perky as the cosmos. But Cousin Leona, I have bad news about the Zoo Doo. It's missing."

"Nonsense, dear. You've just misplaced it."

"I haven't moved it."

"Have you looked in the hydrangeas?"

I don't have hydrangeas. "Honestly, Leona, I haven't touched it. Bitsy thinks it was stolen."

"Does she?" Leona considered this. "She could be right, dear. There's been a rash of petty thefts at the cemetery."

"Bitsy said that was the wind."

"The breezes we've been having could hardly blow away something the general size and weight of a chocolate Chihuahua, dear." She stopped, looking pensive. "Did I just say 'chocolate Chihuahua?'"

"Yes, though I didn't like to draw attention to it."

"Don't be silly, dear. What I meant to say was concrete Chihuahua."

"Why are we even talking about Chihuahuas?"

"Because of the angels, Margaret. Do pay attention. They aren't terribly big and apparently some people like to put them at gravesides along with their flower arrangements. Only, for some reason, they've always struck me as looking more like Chihuahuas. The point is," she said with a rap of her knuckles on the counter because I started snickering, "they're being stolen. Those, and the silly garden gnomes Bud Bowman put in the traffic island over on Maple."

"And you think there's a connection between missing angels, garden gnomes, and my Zoo Doo elephant?"

"Not necessarily, dear. I just find it interesting. Why, for instance, take the gnomes from the traffic island on Maple and not the far more appealing turtles from the city garden on Logan?"

"They're cast iron. Pretty heavy."

"Only the larger ones. The smaller ones are quite portable. Anyway, you should keep better track of your belongings, Margaret. My Zoo Doo elephant is right where it belongs, nestled in my nasturtiums."

"Well, I'm sorry mine is gone."

She patted my hand and left, clucking something about the world and what it's coming to especially in light of my keen interest in gardening. If Leona's wishes were hydrangeas, my interests and gardening might coincide.

Nilda wandered out of the other room with a short stack of cookbooks. Her trade credit wasn't enough to cover the total. On other days, when that happens, she's been quick to put some books back. But today she didn't seem to mind parting with a bit of cash to make up the difference. Her fingers did falter slightly with her wallet, and her parting smile was a tad sickly, but in general she appeared satisfied with her haul.

The rest of the day went as my days tend to go. I operate, for the most part, in a pleasant haze of bookselling. Customers waxed and waned. I parted with three Roald Dahl first editions I'd half planned on adopting as my own. I turned them over to their new owner, one of those customers one occasionally finds standing, as if in a stupor, stroking a book and cooing. How can that kind of passion be denied? It's certainly not within my power to do so.

Leona called in the middle of the afternoon.

"It's a poor joke, Margaret, if that's what you intended. I want my elephant back in my nasturtiums, where it belongs, immediately." She was using her knuckle-rapping voice.

"Your elephant is missing, too?"

"A very poor joke."

"Cousin Leona, I didn't take your elephant. You know I wouldn't tease you like that."

It took several minutes to unruffle her feathers. And, thanks to Bitsy spreading her unpleasant opinions, it also took a promise to ask Ed Tidwell what he might know about pilfered pachyderms. I hated the thought of doing that. Ed is in the habit of calling me darlin' in such a sweet, old-fashioned way that he floats above suspicion in my book. And I take my books seriously.

Leona's call reminded me of the missing copy of the pictorial history. More often than not, a missing book just turns out to be misplaced. Especially a book full of nostalgia such as this one, that invites people to sit in a quiet corner and pour over it. But I didn't spot the pictorial history anywhere as I straightened up around the store throughout the day. I don't get a lot of shop lifting, but it was beginning to look as though this book had walked out the door.

Not with Ed, though, as Bitsy had insisted. And even Bitsy couldn't argue with my proof. She's right. Ed smells. And Ed's smell lingers longer than he does. I knew he hadn't taken the book this morning and my nose knew he hadn't been in the store since before the pictorial history went on sale. Someone else had helped him or herself to it and just as likely to a few other things I hadn't noticed yet.

My appointment to look at Ed's books was for 7:00 that evening, giving me time to close up shop before driving out to the flea market on the four-lane at the edge of town.

The flea market is a year-round junk sale operated by whoever pays for floor space in a couple of barn-like metal buildings. The buildings are saunas in our humid east Tennessee summers and walk-in freezers in winter. Not an ideal environment for storing anything valuable, like the leather bound books and vintage paperbacks Ed had described, but I hoped he was only storing them there temporarily.

The market was closed for the night, but Ed had said some of the flea merchants might be there tending their stock. His battered pickup was in the gravel parking lot, along with a couple of other motley vehicles, when I pulled in. One car, minus wheels and several windows, was up on cinder blocks, perhaps representing some of the quality merchandise available inside.

Weeds encroached on the perimeter of the lot, blurring its edge in the gathering dusk. Some of the heartier specimens of chicory straggled up against the building making a patchy, forlorn foundation planting. Near the door the weeds gave up, abandoning the ground to drifts of cigarette butts and bits of old cellophane wrappers. But even the rust streaks on this tin can of a building couldn't dampen the flicker of excitement I always feel when on the hunt for books.

"Are you coming in darlin', or are you just going to stand there with that moon calf look on your face?" Ed pulled himself out of the shadows by the front door, startling me.

"Sorry, Ed, didn't mean to keep you waiting."

He unlocked the door and I couldn't help grinning as he held it for me.

"Which booth is yours?" I asked. The venue might not be promising, but my fingers were tingling.

"No booth. These books aren't for sale to just any old body. They're locked up safe in the back room. You ever been out here?"

"No."

"Well, we can't be having that, now. We'll take the scenic route."

He led me through a rat warren of knocked together booths and folding tables. Half walls separated some spaces. Panels made of two by fours and chicken wire separated others. We wound our way past odds and ends of furniture, racks of clothes, tables covered in flat cases crammed with earrings, watch fobs, bracelets, junk. My feet slowed at an alcove made of bookcases, but all I saw on the shelves were stacks of *National Geographic* and rows of *Reader's Digest Condensed Books*. I sighed and hurried after Ed who'd almost disappeared around another bend.

"Evening, Ed," I heard someone call from a distance. "You ever going to let me have a look at those books?"

"You've already got enough."

I caught up with him, but didn't see who he'd been answering.

"And that," he whispered, leaning in a little too close for olfactory comfort, "is somebody these books for dang sure ain't for sale to. Like as not rob me blind." He nodded a couple of times to seal his opinion. "Hey, you ever see one of these?" He pointed out a contraption sitting next to a waffle iron. It looked like a Frankenstein-inspired pressure cooker.

"Sorry, I'm not much of a cook."

"Not that kind of cooking, darlin'," he cackled. "It's a vulcanizer for rubber dentures. Hundred, maybe more, years old. Come on." As he set off again, the metal roof creaked. "Wind," he said over his shoulder.

The roof creaked again and softly moaned as the wind found a way under the eaves. Then the lights flickered.

"You got spooks out here, Ed?"

"She don't scare me none."

As I was deciphering this remark, the lights went out altogether.

"Ow."

"Watch you don't bump into anything, darlin'."

"Thanks," I said, rubbing my shin, "Ed, I can't see a thing. Is it the electricity? Maybe we should come back when it's back on."

"You still can't see my books, Nilda," he shouted, startling me. Then he muttered, "It's not the electricity, darlin', it's sour grapes. That woman won't give up. She flipped the lights on her way out and tomorrow she'll pretend she forgot we were here."

"You're kidding. That was Nilda? She's like that?"

"Much good it'll do her. C'mon."

"Ed, it's pitch black."

"But I've got a flashlight. Here," he proved it by shining it in my eyes, then held it out to me, "you probably got steadier hands. Now, let's cut to the chase. C'mon over this way."

The place was more claustrophobic by flashlight, but Ed abandoned the scenic route and we threaded our way quickly to the back of the building. The roof continued to creak and pop, as though settling in for the night. I kept my eyes on Ed's back and my bobbling pool of light.

"Shine it over here."

He fumbled with a padlock securing a hasp on a paint-deprived door. Padlock removed, he swung the door open, grabbed the flashlight from me and played it over the room beyond.

The smell, alone, broke my heart. It was a dungeon with books as derelict and dying prisoners. The room was dirty and damp and there were probably silverfish sliding in and out of the musty pages. I might have sat down and cried if there'd been anyplace to sit other than on the drunken piles of mistreated books. I tried to pull myself together for Ed's sake, but he caught the expression on my face when he swung the flashlight my way.

"What's that mean, Margaret?"

"Oh, Ed."

"But I've looked these things up on the Internet and I know they're worth a mint. Look here at this one. It's a first paperback edition of *Cannery Row*."

He brushed grit off the cover and put it in my hand. It was sticky with mildew. Even with the damp, though, I knew if I tried to open it, the brittle cover would shatter.

"You're not getting a really good look at them, Margaret. I'll run go find the switch for the lights."

"No, Ed, really, I'm sorry."

He was so earnest about the horde, so sure they'd bring a fortune. I've known antiquarian book dealers who would have laid into him up one side and down the other over the abuse of the books. One old guy in Knoxville would have pelted him with them and then gone to find stones to finish the job properly. I was tempted to just take a shovel and bury the poor dead things.

"Well, hell, Margaret," he said, summing it up.

"Sorry, Ed," I said again. I handed the corpse of *Cannery Row* back to him and wiped my hand on my jeans, hoping I'd remember to run them through the washer about ten times when I got home. "Whose are they, by the way?"

"Doesn't much matter, does it? Unless you're selling me a load of bull. You aiming to go behind my back, cut me out?"

"No, Ed."

"Some would. Well," he shone the light around one more time, tossed the Steinbeck on the nearest pile, and heaved a sigh.

"I'm really sorry, Ed."

"So you said. You think if I put them out in the sun for awhile? Maybe dry them out in a slow oven?"

"No."

He grunted.

"Sorry."

We started back to the front door, Ed hunched, shambling, and dejected, me wondering why I couldn't think of anything more helpful to say than 'sorry'.

"Whoa, sorry, Ed."

I'd run smack into the smelly bulk of him when he stopped short. We untangled ourselves and I was mildly amused to see him brush himself off.

"I forgot to lock up," he said. "Wait here."

I looked around at the dark shapes and darker shadows and listened to the roof noises and the wind under the eaves.

"I'll come with you," I called, hurrying after him. I was beginning to really dislike this place. At least he was conscientious. I'd just leave the door unlocked and hope someone would steal the whole sorry mess.

We rounded a corner and Ed stopped short again. By executing some fancy footwork, I avoided running into him this time. He looked unimpressed, but surprised me with a pirouette of his own, pulling me with him back around the corner.

"Ssh," he said. "There's someone there."

He pulled me further around the corner, into one of the alcoves, and sank to the floor.

"Ed, it's probably just someone else Nilda left in the dark."

"Yeah, well, whoever it is, is in the back room, throwing the books around."

"Then let's tiptoe out of here and call the police."

"Let's call them right now." He pulled a cell phone out of a pocket.

"You've got a cell phone?"

"It's the twenty first century, Margaret."

"Sure, sorry."

"Here, hold the flashlight. Keep it low."

"Okay."

"Keep it low, but shine it over here so I can see to dial, okay?"

"Sorry. But it's hard to see where you're pointing in the pitch black."

"Which is why you shine the light on me and not on whatever else attracts your wandering eye."

"Sorry."

"And stop…"

"…And I'll stop saying sorry." I waited two beats then added, "Sorry." Which gave me time, while Ed muttered and swore, to contemplate what I'd seen when the flashlight strayed. Angels?

And elephants. "Ed, whose booth is this?"

By now he was whispering urgently into the phone so I relegated him to the dark and flashed the light under the table we were crouched behind. What was all this stuff doing here?

A gnome peeked at me from between the wings of two angels, and a Zoo Doo elephant, my Zoo Doo elephant sat in a nest of newspapers off in the corner. I knew it was mine, because Leona's, complete with a lei of withered nasturtiums, was in a box sitting on… I crawled under the table and lifted the elephant out of the box. Yes, there was the missing copy of *A Pictorial History of Greater Stonewall*.

"Well, I'll be damned."

That wasn't me and it wasn't Ed. I froze.

"What are you doing in my booth, Ed?" It was Nilda.

She had a flashlight trained on him. I stayed where I was, out of sight under the table.

"I thought you left when Margaret did."

"I came back to lock up my books," he said, getting to his feet. "Got a little disoriented in the dark."

"Yeah, well you got a little disoriented with those books, too, didn't you? Bunch of crap," she jeered.

I felt craven, not helping Ed out. But as long as Nilda didn't know I was hiding there with her loot, maybe he could waltz his way out and I could sashay after him, when the coast was clear.

"I called the cops," said Ed.

So much for waltzing out.

"Am I supposed to be scared? I'm a businesswoman. You're the local crackpot. Who do you think they're going to believe? Face reality. I'm leaving."

She meant the caustic pep talk for Ed, but it hit me right between the eyes.

"Hold it, Nilda," I said, scrambling out from under the table. "Ed is not a crackpot. I'm a businesswoman. And you're a thief." I had a Zoo Doo elephant in each hand to prove it and shook them at her. "And the cops will be plenty interested to see what else you've got stashed away here."

The lights came on. Authoritative voices and solid footsteps made their way toward us.

Nilda turned and sprinted, but Ed stuck his foot out just in time.

"Watch your step, darlin'," he said.

"Ed Tidwell? A hero? You're right, I don't believe it." Bitsy, my constant and unrelenting sister, was waiting for me on the steps when I got home.

"Every word is true, darlin'," I said, using Ed's endearment to good effect on her. It did interesting things to her eyebrows.

She trailed me inside and upstairs as I shed layers on my way to the shower. My clothes and possibly my skin, hair, teeth, and bones had absorbed more of the essence of Ed than I would have thought possible.

"Bitsy, give me ten minutes in the shower and then I will explain all," I said, closing the bathroom door in her face. "Why don't you go make some cocoa?"

It was more like fifteen minutes later, wrapped in my big blue bathrobe and still toweling my hair, that I joined her in the kitchen. And Leona, I discovered as I emerged from the towel. They were sipping cocoa. Bitsy eyed me over the rim of her mug as though seeing something more exotic than a Zoo Doo elephant. Leona was finishing the crossword puzzle I'd been saving for bedtime.

"So, let me get this straight," Bitsy said, "this customer of yours, Willy or Nilly or…"

"Nilda."

"She took the elephants, and she's responsible for the thefts at the cemetery, and she stole Bud Bowman's garden gnome?"

"And she helped herself regularly to my books, including the pictorial history. She shoplifted as many books as she ever bought," I said, helping myself to the cocoa and leaning against the kitchen counter. "And it's no wonder the books she brought in for trade looked so good, because she stole them from someone else in the first place. She's been a one woman crime wave keeping two flea market booths in two separate towns stocked. The one here with stuff she picked up over in Bristol, and the one in Bristol with stuff she stole here. And Ed's the hero of the hour."

"I don't see how you figure that," Bitsy said.

"He's practically a Boy Scout, Bitsy, prepared for every contingency. Flashlight, cell phone, who knows what else he keeps handy in those pockets of his."

"What do you suppose they mean by 'triple-time tripping' and what's an eight letter word for it?" Leona asked.

"Fandango," I said, twirling, then doing a little two or maybe a three-step over to the table. "Tripping the light fantastic. Come to think of it, that's how Ed caught Nilda. He's pretty handy with his feet, too."

"Nonsense," Bitsy said.

"Bitsy, dear, that's hardly charitable of you. You weren't there this evening," Leona said.

"I mean, I thought fandango meant nonsense." She smiled sweetly. "Like some stories."

"Why, I believe you're right, dear. And, Margaret, you say we'll get our Zoo Doo back?"

"Eventually. Right now the elephants are evidence."

"That's fine then. Now, what's a ten letter word for booster, beginning with p and ending with f?"

"Try two words; petty thief."

"Of course. And there we are," she said, pocketing my pencil. "All done." She folded the crossword and tossed it into the recycling bin. "Bitsy, why don't you walk me home? Good night, Margaret, dear."

"Good night, Cousin Leona."

"By the way, Margaret," Bitsy said, turning at the door, "you didn't mention Ed's books. Were they worth looking at?"

"Bitsy, they were indescribable, incredible, unbelievable. They were staggering. They left me breathless. They brought tears to my eyes…"

"Don't make yourself dizzy, Margaret."

"Good night, Bitsy."

The possum in this story is another relic from my childhood. Dad was planning to show my brothers and me how to do taxidermy, something he'd never actually done himself. We had a roadkill possum in the freezer, a power outage, good neighbors... and another good case of "what if?"

Practically Perfect

My sister, Bitsy, thinks I'm afraid of marriage. Her latest theory is that I attach what affection I spare from my bookstore to my sometimes-dear-one, Gene, because he's safe. She figures no one in her right mind would marry him. I don't know about that. But I see what she goes through to maintain her life, married and on an even keel, and know that I'm not ready to take my place beside her as a pillar of wedded perfection. I salute her efforts, ignore her retorts, and move on. I'm a realist.

"Margaret, you live in such a fantasy world." That was Bitsy, aggrieved on this sun-dappled day and come to spread her affliction.

I put down the copy of *The Diary of Samuel Pepys* I was reading. Face up, so she might enjoy the irony of her words as much as I. It was an idle wish.

"Here you are, lolling in the sun, lost in another book, a glass of iced tea at your elbow. It must be nice."

It was. It was the first warm day this spring and the first afternoon I'd taken off in three months, leaving my business in the hands of a new but able employee. I run a combination new and used bookstore in my old house. The books and I have a symbiotic relationship. They take up most of the downstairs and keep the bread on my kitchen table. I take up some of the upstairs and do my best to make the books feel at home as long as they're with me. If that includes taking Sam Pepys out for a little sunshine on my afternoon off, I'm happy to oblige.

"What's up, Bitsy? Like some tea?"

"I don't think I could possibly swallow anything. I'm just so…" She stretched that single syllable out as though preparing to launch an aria. Then she peered closely at the seat of my other Adirondack for anything icky that might transfer to her beautifully pressed slacks before dumping herself into it. "I truly don't know how I am. And you've been so wrapped up in your own little book world that you probably haven't heard the news, have you?"

"Something tragic has happened?"

"Margaret, Barb's husband was killed by a hit and run driver."

"Oh my god." Barb is one of my least favorite of Bitsy's friends. She's a bad influence on Bitsy, encouraging her to do things like wear seasonal sweatshirts with glitter on them. She's also never bought a book from me. But even that didn't mean she deserved to have her life shattered this way. "Bitsy, that's awful. How is she?"

"That's the worst part. She's happy about it!"

"Oh, no, that must be shock. Sometimes it affects people in strange ways."

"'Good riddance to jerks I've known' were her exact words. She thinks it was some kind of karmic wish fulfillment. Did you know they'd been seeing a marriage counselor?"

I shook my head.

"Well, I didn't either and here I thought she and I were best friends. She says the counselor took her aside after only three sessions and told her there was no help for Herb, that he was a hopeless narcissist who would never change, and that really the best thing Barb could hope for was for him to be hit by a bus."

"Are they allowed to say things like that?"

"You wouldn't think so, would you?"

"Maybe they are if it's true. Actually it's kind of a refreshing attitude."

"Margaret!"

"Well, think about it, Bitsy. Aren't those radio and TV self-help gurus always encouraging people to be honest about their feelings? And haven't marriage counselors got feelings, too?"

Bitsy rolled her eyes.

"You don't think Barb did it, do you?"

She stopped her eyes mid-roll and gave me the full benefit of their laser-like burn. "How can you even suggest such a thing?"

"Stranger things have happened, and you've got to admit, it was awfully convenient."

"Why do I ever think you're the right person to come to in a crisis?" She started to rise in her indignation.

"What crisis? It just sounds pretty sad all the way around."

"And that's just it." She collapsed again, not unlike the last cheese soufflé I attempted. "It is so sad. And then, the really worst part is, how does one comfort the grieving widow when the widow is celebrating with champagne?" She concluded with a small noise that I wouldn't want to try duplicating.

But it touched me. Poor Bitsy. I might not be ready for marriage, but a happy state of wedded bliss is her *raison d'être*. She would stand tall on any pedestal erected for the Goddess of Connubiality and at the same time she'd be whipping up a batch of biscotti and planning the next Garden Club meeting.

And now here she was, mourning the shambles of her best friend's literally dead marriage and hung up on the horns of an etiquette dilemma. I thought about nipping into the bookstore to consult Emily Post or Miss Manners for her. Instead I picked up Pepys again. I'd just been reading something interesting from November 1665.

"How about this, Bitsy. Invite Barb over for one of your really nice dinners, round the table out with a few other people she knows, and then all of you simply offer her your continuing support and friendship."

"You think?"

"I do."

She narrowed her eyes. "You're not just making fun of this situation?"

"No. In fact, no less an authority than Samuel Pepys would applaud the gesture. You want to know what he had to say?" Her eyebrows gave a tentative answer. "He said: 'Strange to see how a good dinner and feasting reconciles everybody.' See?"

"Well, there's no arguing the 'strange' in this case. But, you know, I think maybe you're right. In fact, I'm going to do it. Thank you, Margaret."

"You're welcome."

"And now I think I will have that glass of tea. No, no, don't get up. I'll help myself."

I closed my eyes and drank in the placid, sun-drenched silence. Dealing with Bitsy's crises takes cunning and can be exhausting. Thanks to good old Sam Pepys, though, this one had been fairly smooth sailing. I was just having a quiet guffaw over how differently things might have turned out if instead of Pepys I'd been reading Kinky Friedman, when I heard Bitsy bugling something in the kitchen. Now what?

"Margaret! Catastrophe!"

I opened my eyes to see Bitsy standing in the doorway like some martyred saint of the deep freeze, arms outstretched, holding dripping, half-melted packages of unidentifiable frozen foods.

"I can't believe you didn't notice this earlier, Margaret. Your freezer is having a melt down!"

So much for the rest of my afternoon off.

"And apparently there are no leads. It was hit and run, no witnesses. Just splat and no more Herb Buchanan," I said, shaking my head.

"That's simply dreadful, dear. But was she able to get it all into her own freezer?"

"Hm? Oh, you mean Bitsy." Our elderly cousin, Leona, had tottered over from her house next door as soon as the coast and my freezer were clear. She likes to maintain the fiction of uncanny coincidence when it comes to the timing between Bitsy's departures and her own arrivals. She'd undoubtedly been watching the frozen food transfer from behind her lace curtain. "Yes, she got it all, amid much wailing and moaning and gnashing of her teeth."

"Don't be ungrateful, dear."

"Oh, I'm completely grateful, Cousin Leona. She came to the rescue just in time, as she so often does. In fact, I was thinking we should design a family crest in her honor. Bitsy, mounted, rampant and triumphant. What do you think?"

"I think sometimes you're very wicked."

"I don't know, if it were tastefully done…"

"I hate to interrupt, dear, but I didn't just come over for a cup of tea and your usual blather. I seem to have misplaced my county map and I was wondering if you have one."

Leona has lived in our small town all her life and knows the network of county roads as intimately as she knows her own 80-year-old wrinkles.

"You need a map?"

"Have you called the repairman yet?"

"Hm? Oh, yeah, he'll be here sometime between 8am and 8pm someday between Monday and Friday either this week or next. So, do you want a road map or the one that shows where all the old grist mills and post offices and one room school houses were located?" Her eyes lit up.

"Did Grace finally finish that map for the Historical Society?"

"Yeah, they're pretty neat. You want one? A bargain at only $12.95."

"Good heavens. And you have them in the bookstore?" I nodded. "Then there's no need for me to buy one. No, a road map will do just fine."

Leona has reached a difficult age, not yet ready to relinquish her driver's license but not as steady behind the wheel as she used to be. It's a ticklish subject to broach with someone who's been independent all her life.

"I thought you were sticking close to home these days," I said carefully. "You know, curtailing the driving?"

"Did you have to throw anything out, dear?"

I was getting a little fatigued following the bouncing ball of this conversation. "No, the chocolate chip cookie dough ice cream was a near miss, though, so we ate it."

"That's nice, dear. Now, the map?"

I swallowed the rest of my tea, regarding her through narrowed eyes, a move that always unnerves me when Bitsy does it. It had no effect on Leona, though. She sipped her own tea, beamed around at my sunny yellow kitchen and ignored me and my questions.

After I fetched the map for her, I watched as she crossed our yards to her own back door. I've come to realize over the years that, although Leona is essentially an honest little old lady, she isn't entirely trustworthy. What was she up to, now, I wondered? And why was she being evasive?

That evening I went over to Bitsy's to visit my refrozen refugees and thank her again for putting her own freezer in chaos on my behalf.

"Margaret, I can't believe you don't label everything you put in your freezer."

I shrugged. "Most of it's in the original containers, Bitsy."

"But the leftovers, Margaret. They're all in recycled plastic packages. How do you tell the difference between a tub of tuna noodle casserole and Cool Whip?"

"It's a knack," I said. What I didn't dare tell her was that some of the packages we'd transferred to her freezer might as well have been complete strangers to me. What was that thing wrapped in aluminum foil the size and shape of a recumbent toy poodle?

Bitsy's house is always orderly. The chairs at her kitchen table tuck themselves demurely beneath it. The top of her refrigerator glistens. Her spice jars march in alphabetical order. Her freezer is heavily labeled and probably unionized. All afternoon I'd pictured her pint containers of zucchini puree turning up their noses at my poor rescued souls. Whatever they were.

"I really do appreciate you doing this, Bitsy. You know, you're welcome to use any of it you want to."

"If I could identify any of it for certain, I might."

Ordinarily I expect a statement like that to come out on the snippy side. But this one wasn't up to her usual snide standards. She sounded preoccupied, a trifle flat. I tried nudging her back into her groove.

"Oh, don't worry about that, Bitsy. Just throw caution to the winds, choose something at random and call it 'adventures in fine dining'. That's what I do."

But she only sighed.

"This thing with Barb is really getting you down, isn't it?"

"Yeah, I went to see her again this afternoon, to invite her for our dinner tomorrow night."

Our dinner?

We'd moved into her living room, where I left footprints in the freshly vacuumed pile of her carpet. She sprawled in an overstuffed armchair. Very un-Bitsy-like. I took my shoes off and tucked my feet under me on the sofa opposite her.

"It's tomorrow night, by the way. Did I tell you that? I probably didn't. You can be here, though, can't you? Oh, I'm a mess. Margaret, why should I be more upset about Herb than Barb is? Do you know what her marriage counselor says? He was there this afternoon. Making a condolence call that hardly seemed necessary. He said he encourages people to go out and do something positive when they're feeling troubled. He said it doesn't really matter what you do. Just the doing can be good for improving one's outlook."

"Sounds reasonable, I suppose," I said.

"It sounds like a shoe commercial."

"Well, you helped me in my hour of freezer need, Bitsy. That was something positive. How did that make you feel?"

"It didn't help."

"Maybe the dinner tomorrow night will. Who else is coming?"

"Chuck."

"Who's Chuck?"

"The marriage counselor. Barb invited him." She gazed out the front window, then, temporarily lost in seductive melancholy. The sound of the fishing show her husband, Rodney, was watching in the den drifted lazily by in the background. When she spoke again, her voice was hollow and came as though from a long way off. "Do you know what I gave Rodney for supper tonight? Canned soup."

If that didn't tell me everything I needed to know about her state of mind, her next sigh and statement did.

"I invited Gene for tomorrow night, too."

Bitsy never willingly invites Gene anywhere, much less by calling him up personally. As for referring to him as anything other than 'what's-his-name,' well, this was serious and it was a good thing I'd stopped by. I had just the distraction she needed to get her up and doing again for her own good.

A glowing point of harmony in our otherwise sisterly relationship is our mutual interest in the wonder that is Leona's aging mind. Leona can be exasperating, but mostly we find ourselves in awe of her continuing ability to manipulate the world around her to her complete satisfaction. I told Bitsy, now, about Leona's odd behavior over the map. At first I wasn't sure she'd heard me. Then her head swiveled around toward me, her eyes refocused. Good.

"I knew you'd think there was something fishy about the way she kept changing the subject," I said.

"What do you suppose she's up to?"

"I was hoping you could figure that out."

Bitsy's spine straightened. "I think you should start checking her odometer."

"What?"

"Well, I can't do everything, Margaret. Not only do I have to work around your motley collection of frozen foods but, in case you've forgotten, I'm also putting on a dinner party tomorrow night. We need to find out if Leona's out there racking up the miles, endangering the population by driving all over creation. In fact, you should check her front bumper. For all we know she's the one who hit poor Herb and now she's looking for some out of the way place to dump her car before the police get on to her."

Bitsy is amazing. She wasn't even breathing hard after that.

"Have you noticed her car gone more than usual, lately?" She asked.

"Well, I've been pretty busy in the store."

"In other words, you haven't been paying attention. You need to check her odometer. Do it every night after you see her lights go out. After all, Margaret, you're the one who keeps harping on about how she probably shouldn't even be driving these days."

This call to arms and rush to hyperbolic action was so typically Bitsy. Obviously she was going to be all right. I left her buffing the light bulbs in the chandelier over her dining room table and muttering through her mental filing system in search of something appropriate to serve tomorrow night.

Of course, that left me with the problem of whether or not I should actually follow Bitsy's directive. Should I check Leona's odometer? But I was curious, too, and the deed itself took no particularly clandestine skills. Her car sits in her driveway between her house and mine. I waited until her bedroom light went out, strolled over with my mini flashlight, peered in through the driver's side window and scribbled down the numbers. Perfectly simple.

"You didn't really do that, did you?" Gene asked the next morning.

We have an on again, off again, relationship which has been more on the on-ish side lately and means he stops by most mornings for a shot of caffeine and a canoodle.

"I did, but I didn't inhale."

"But it's an invasion of her privacy."

I got out his favorite mug while he did his best to invade my privacy by putting his arms around me and nuzzling my left ear. For safety's sake, I waited until he was finished before pouring the coffee. The mug he likes has the floor plan of a Frank Lloyd Wright house on it and when you pour in something hot the floor plan disappears and a picture of the completed house takes its place. The mug is almost as entertaining as the guy who swigs his coffee from it.

"So you don't see checking up on Leona as doing something positive in troubling circumstances?" I asked, when once again we were seated at the kitchen table.

"Positively crackers, maybe. You two don't seriously think Leona ran over Herb, do you?"

"I don't. And, really, Bitsy probably doesn't either. But I'll tell you what's got icy fingers creeping up and down my spine."

"I've got toasty fingers that wouldn't mind creeping up and down your spine." He wiggled his eyebrows and the fingers in question. I did my best to ignore them.

"It's this shoebox philosophy Chuck the marriage counselor is peddling. What if he's been pushing that on Barb all along and she finally decided to follow his advice, only in a really final kind of way?"

"A neat combination of 'just do it' and 'do it yourself'? Yeah, I can see the infomercial for it now," he said. "Has your marriage gone flat but not flat enough? Try Barbie's Hubby Bumper and we guarantee, he'll be in seventh heaven and so will you."

"Yeah, something like that."

"So, you going to go check Barb's front bumper?"

"Eeuw. But what do you think?"

"That the police have probably already checked it, unhappy spouses being prime suspects."

"Good point. Well," I shook myself to dislodge the icy digits still clinging to my spine, "how's the work going on the museum?"

And he was off. Gene is in love with his work and any discussion of whatever his current project happens to be turns into a piece of performance art. I slid his still half-full mug away from the flying hands and sat back to watch.

Gene was an itinerant architect until he settled down here. He specializes in redesigning existing buildings. If he had a motto it might be 'recycling through reasonable redesigns'. But that sounds so much like one of the perky slogans Bitsy flings at my bookstore from time to time that I've never suggested it to him. He's working now with a civic group that's turning the old brick Mayflower warehouse into a children's museum.

"I'll hire a child to take me there when it opens," I said when he'd subsided. "Where are all the exhibits coming from?"

"Combination of sources but through donations mostly. They even got a permit for volunteers to pick up roadkill that's still in reasonable shape and a taxidermist is working with them so they'll have a study collection of indigenous fauna."

"Roadkill, mmm, yummy. And that brings us back nicely to poor flat Herb. Hey, maybe that's what happened to him. An over-zealous volunteer mistook him for a warthog, couldn't believe her luck and ran him down without double-checking to see if warthogs are indigenous. And that theory has the added benefit of letting Leona off the hook because she knows warthogs don't grow around here." I stopped to take a sip of coffee. "What? What's that look on your face?"

It was an interesting look. Not quite guilty, not quite sneaky. But definitely not open and honest. It kind of reminded me of Leona.

"Okay," he said, "promise you won't tell Leona I told you?"

"Told me what and why shouldn't I know?"

"She didn't want you to worry. And she didn't want Bitsy to rail."

"With that lead in, I think you'd better go ahead and tell me."

"Leona is one of the volunteers picking up roadkill for the museum. She says she sees it as a good recycling effort and a far nobler end for the animals than being scraped up by some county road crew. And she says it gives her a reason to hop out of bed each morning. Better pickings first thing in the morning, apparently. So that's probably why she wanted the map. They're supposed to keep track of where they pick something up and what with new roads and new road names and missing road signs, well, you get the picture."

"And a lovely picture it is, too. Little old Leona up to her elbows in fresh roadkill."

"She doesn't pick up messy ones. She got a great wood duck last week." He stopped, head cocked, looking at me. "It doesn't bother you that she's doing it, does it?"

"No."

"I told her it wouldn't."

"The logistics of it leave me wondering, though. How do you pick up a dead wood duck? By the beak? By the feet? One of those things I never thought I'd have to think about. Well, it's a peculiar hobby, but if it puts a spring in her step, why not? But I do worry about her driving back roads early in the morning. What if she has car trouble? What if she gets lost?"

"What if I told you that I've been driving her?"

"Have you?"

He shrugged and acknowledged sheepishly that he had.

"Well, that's very sweet of you and please don't ever ask me if I want to come along for the ride. But, so, uh, where does Leona put her flat friends after she picks them up?"

"Freezer. Then every couple of weeks someone from the museum picks them up."

"Good thing Bitsy took all my stuff over to her house, then. I'd hate to get my tuna noodle casserole mixed up with dead duck surprise."

Over another cup of coffee we made our plans for meeting up later and wending our way over to Bitsy's condolence dinner. Then we canoodled a bit more and Gene trailed off to his office and his drawing board and I went to flip the open sign on the front door and start my business day.

Tragedy often translates into better book business. People come looking for words they've found comforting in the past, wanting to share them with someone else who is hurting. The words are in essays and poetry, fables or prayers. Some people find them in meditations, others hold onto the simplicity of a beautiful children's picture book.

"Margaret, have you got any books about getting on with your life now that someone else's is over?"

"Barb?"

"Yeah, it's me. I bet you didn't recognize me, did you?"

"No." Besides showing up in the bookstore, which for her is an alien environment, she'd dyed her mousy brown hair screaming Lucy red. Although maybe the words on her black sweatshirt should have given me a clue. They said, 'He's dead. Get over it.'

"Barb, I'm sorry about Herb."

"Thank you, Margaret. You're so sweet. But I'm not going to pretend that it wasn't for the best." She delivered a well-choreographed sigh and dismissive little shrug of her shoulders, then reapplied her perky smile. "Now, where would you have a book like that, because I promised Chuck I'd at least take a look and he's been such a rock through all this that I feel like I kind of owe him that much. Chuck's a great believer in self-help."

"That's what I hear. Well, let's go take a look."

I led her over into the nonfiction section, wondering which books to nudge her toward, bereavement and spirituality or the psychology books for the more seriously loony. The decision was taken out of my hands, though, when a used copy of *Jane Fonda's Workout Book* caught her eye and sidetracked her before we got anywhere near a book she might really need. I could definitely see why Bitsy was having trouble dealing with this behavior. But, as far as I could see, if Barb was feeling happily liberated from the hard work of being married to a narcissistic moron, who was I to tsk-tsk in her direction? I left her trying out some of Jane's moves and went to help other customers.

But during a lull I couldn't quite help myself and I sidled over toward the windows to cast an eye over the bumpers parked in front of the store. Being liberated is one thing. How one gets that way is something else. And even though Bitsy vouched for Barb's sense of right and wrong, and Gene trusted the police to look in all the obvious places, I needed to see for myself.

All bumpers appeared to be unbumped.

Which left me with an interesting bit of self-observation. Looking out at that row of faultless bumpers, I realized I was disappointed. I actually wanted to think Barb ran down Herb. Was that somehow sick? Should it bother me?

"Gotta run, Margaret." Barb was waving her fingertips at me. "See you tonight at Bitsy's. Bye!" she trilled and skipped out the door. *Sans* a single damn book.

So, no, it didn't bother me that I wanted to think Barb capable of death by Dodge. It was a normal, healthy reaction on my part to someone who never reads or buys books.

"Margaret, at last! I'm running behind."

Bitsy met us at the door waving a spatula and an industrial-sized potholder. Ordinarily she's the unflappable major general of her kitchen. Not so this evening. She stopped mid-flap when she saw Gene behind me. "Oh. Hi. Rodney's in the living room. Why don't you join him?"

"Sure I can't give you a hand with anything?" he asked.

"No thanks." She watched as he retreated to the other room, then she started flapping again. "Margaret, I forgot the bread. I meant to pick up one of those loaves of walnut bread at the bakery this afternoon but it went clear out of my head when I heard.... Well, here, come in the kitchen and I'll tell you while I finish up."

I started to sit down, ready to be agog at whatever had her in her latest tizzy.

"Wait!" she turned on me with her spoon. "I just remembered. I have a loaf of that bread in the freezer. Run downstairs and get it, will?"

"Sure."

"Oh, thank goodness. The quiche is ready to come out of the oven and you can just pop the bread in and disaster will be averted."

I left her dealing severely with whatever was threatening to boil over on the stove and headed for the basement where she keeps her freezer in all its labeled glory. Bitsy could, with confidence, ask even the queen of England to fetch something from her basement. That's because Bitsy's basement is as highly polished as the rest of her house.

In fact, I found two loaves of the bread, one labeled, one not. Was this a chink in Bitsy's armor? No, on closer inspection, the second loaf turned out to be one of my own mystery packages. And that was probably why I hadn't recognized it yesterday. Such wonderful bread doesn't usually survive long enough at my house to wind up wrapped and frozen. But at times I surprise myself with spurts of self-control and here, obviously, was one of the happy results. I weighed both loaves in my hands and came to a decision. I headed back upstairs with mine.

Some things are so satisfying. Showing one's sister that hers is not the only route to happiness is one. I might not wax my basement steps or rule my freezer with an iron fist, but my frozen food is no less flavorful for that. I handed the bread to Bitsy.

"Good, you already took the label off. And did you know that I always wrap an item for the freezer so that it can go straight into the oven if that's what I want to do with it?" she asked, popping the loaf in the oven.

"Yes, thanks, ever since you melted the plastic wrap on my lasagna I've been doing that too. So, what's up?" I asked, starting to sit down again, "what did you hear that put you in such a muddle?"

"Wait! Come stir this, will you?"

"Sure." I got up again and took over stirring.

She tasted the sauce in another pan, added a *soupçon* of something, re-tasted it and looked satisfied. Then she turned to me, brandishing the spoon.

"Margaret, I'm appalled! No, not at you, keep stirring. But you'll never guess what I heard this afternoon about Leona."

Just then, over Bitsy's shoulder and her menacing spoon, I saw an old VW minibus pull into her driveway. The driver leaned briefly on the horn and it played a riff of 'I Did it My Way'.

"Good god," I said. "Who's that?"

Emotions warred over Bitsy's face.

"Barb and Chuck," she finally said. Taking a deep breath, she handed me her spoon and headed for the door, quavering for Rodney to join her in greeting their guests.

"Did you get a load of that guy?" Gene asked, slipping into the kitchen.

"Shh. No, but I saw what he drives and heard his idea of car horn chic. What's he look like?"

"Fred MacMurray on speed."

As I tried bringing that image into focus, the man himself appeared in the kitchen door.

"Hi. Chuck Overbay. Nice to meet you." He stuck the pipe he held in his right hand between his smiling teeth then stuck the hand out for us to shake. I considered sticking the spoon in my mouth in order to take his hand but decided against it. "Smells great in here. This is a fine thing you people are doing. I just thought I'd tell you that."

Hands now jammed in the pockets of his cardigan, he took a stroll around the kitchen, smiling and nodding at what he saw. He settled himself at the kitchen table, legs crossed at the knee, pipe clamped between his still smiling teeth. Bitsy came rushing back in but stopped short on seeing him.

"Oh, Chuck, wouldn't you rather join Barb and Rodney in the living room? You'll find a plate of veggies and my special zucchini dip in there."

Chuck patted his stomach. "Watching my weight. I'll be happy with the main course. You go right ahead with what you're doing, though. Don't mind me."

She gave a wavering sort of smile. I handed her spoon back and she turned toward the stove.

"But how are you doing, Bitsy?"

She pivoted back to Chuck who continued smiling and talking around his pipe.

"I'm not getting the feeling of ease I expected to find here in the kitchen with you. There appears to be something troubling your mind and I think you'll be more comfortable if you just get it out in the open. I'm sure you'll feel better if you do. I know this unburdening doesn't come naturally to everyone. It takes practice. Remember what I told you yesterday afternoon? Practice the positive. So, now, you go ahead, let it out and we won't mind at all, will we?" He beamed around at Gene and me. "That's what we're here for."

A quick look at Gene and Bitsy proved I wasn't the only one wondering if this guy was for real.

"Well," Bitsy hesitated, casting anxious glances between the pots on the stove, Gene, Chuck, and me.

It was easy money guessing what Bitsy had heard about Leona this afternoon. I tried to head her off. "Bitsy, right before dinner might not be the best time to bring this up. Pun intended."

"Nonsense," said smiling Chuck. "Really. Go ahead. It works."

"Well, ..." She'd been about to burst with the news, anyway, so for Bitsy there was no resisting a green light like that one. "I don't want to upset Barb," she said in what passes for a whisper in her vocal repertoire, "and I don't want to name names. But I received some disturbing information this afternoon." She tiptoed to the kitchen door and looked out. Apparently Barb was safely out of earshot in the living room. "Information about roadkill and someone we know."

Gene shot me an accusatory look.

"She spoke to a witness," I said, shrugging.

"Unimpeachable," Bitsy added. "And I think, Margaret and Gene, that the three of us are going to have to tackle this situation."

"You want us to wrestle this roadkill culprit to the ground?" Gene asked.

I knew Gene had meant it sarcastically but his question had a curious effect on Chuck. In fact, Chuck had shown increasing unease throughout our conversation. But maybe that was because there was an odd smell beginning to float around the periphery of the savory aromas of quiche and the other good things Bitsy had simmering on the stove. It was something vaguely pleasant, but just as vaguely not so pleasant. I was about to suggest to Bitsy that she return her attention to the cooking and leave the rest of our discussion for later when Rodney stuck his head in the door.

"Hon? Need me to take the meat out of the oven for you? It's starting to smell kind of..." and he left it at that because Bitsy was already slamming open the oven door and pulling out the foil-wrapped loaf of bread.

Then Barb trailed in. "I'm sorry," she sniffled. "I was sitting in there all alone for a minute and it suddenly hit me. I *am* all alone. My Honey-Herb is gone." And she sat down at the table and dissolved into tears.

I expected Chuck to make some kind of move to comfort poor Barb but he only had eyes for Bitsy and the bread she'd unwrapped. Which turned out not to be a loaf of that wonderful walnut bread after all.

"What is this?" she asked, poking at it with the end of a spoon.

"Looks like revenge of the roadkill," Gene said.

"Roadkill?" She recoiled, and that really wasn't a healthy color she'd turned.

"What exactly is it?" Rodney whispered to Gene over the top of Bitsy's head. She had buried her face in Rodney's chest and was quietly having hysterics.

"Roadkill?" wailed Barb. "That's what my poor Herb is. And I liked being married to him and, even if he was a narcissist, I loved him. Who would do such a thing? Who would?"

"Woodchuck," said Gene.

"He must have been a very peculiar man," Leona said. This from the 80 year old with an eye for fresh roadkill and a penchant for housing stray members of her collection in my freezer without letting me know.

It was later that evening and Gene and I were tucking the last of my frozen food into Leona's freezer. After Bitsy's abbreviated bereavement bash, my vacating her freezer seemed like the best thing for all concerned.

"He was carried away with his own philosophy, anyway," I said. "Right up to the end, as a matter of fact. He kept telling everyone they'd feel better if they'd just go ahead and do something so I hope he felt better after breaking down and confessing like that."

"I'm pretty sure Barb felt better after slugging him," Gene said. "And Bitsy sure felt better after throwing the woodchuck at him."

"Hmph. No telling when I'll find another woodchuck half so nice as that one was," Leona said. "He was practically perfect."

"That's what Barb was blubbering about Herb when Rodney finally drove her home," I said. "So Bitsy's view of married life is redeemed and she'll be back on familiar ground offering sympathy and comfort to Barb."

Of course she'd have to get over the trauma of serving up a less than perfect dinner first. I was wondering how long I'd be hearing about that little faux pas when I realized Leona was prodding us toward the door with an unsubtle elbow and exaggerated yawns.

"Oh, sorry Leona, we're keeping you up. Thanks for the freezer space," I said. And I kissed her goodnight, which is something I ought to do more often.

Gene gave her a smooch, too.

"Hmph. Really. What am I going to do with you two?"

"How about hitting the road with us extra early tomorrow morning and we'll see what we can do about replacing the woodchuck?" I said.

Her fierce spinster look receeded. "You two are very good to me." Then her sly spinster look slipped in. "You're very good for each other, too. I hope you know that."

"We're working on it," I said.

And taking Gene by the arm, we made our way across the backyard to my place to put in a little more practice.

Margaret can't cook, but that doesn't stop her form idolizing Julia Child. She can't help being suspicious of Bitsy's latest project, either, but that doesn't stop her from once again saying yes. I wrote this story before cell phones were commonplace.

Being Julia

I've always wanted to be Julia Child. This, despite three facts. One, I don't spend much time in the kitchen unless I'm in my pajamas galvanizing my brain with a cup of coffee and the morning crossword. Two, I'm shorter than Julia probably was by age ten. Three, I can't cook. Although in the interest of full disclosure, that third fact is supplied by my sister, Bitsy. Bitsy was born with twice the culinary genes of an ordinary human and arrived in this world with an entire wardrobe of aprons, none of which she ever wears over pajamas.

"A little sci-fi fantasy reading, Margaret?" Bitsy asked the other morning, catching me as I flipped through a magazine between customers.

"Just keeping current." I re-shelved the *Gourmet* I'd been careful not to drool on. I have a small but interesting selection of glossy magazines for sale alongside the new and used titles in my bookshop. And, though I have only a nodding acquaintance with the stove in my kitchen or the weeds in my garden, I know which of my books or magazines to recommend for a brilliant mango salsa or tips on caring for cosmos. "Have you ever heard of ginger chocolate pound cake? There's a recipe for it in that issue."

Bitsy hesitated at the magazine rack.

"It looks like a killer combination of crystallized and fresh ginger," I said over my shoulder, heading for the sales counter.

"How much ginger?" Her eyes lost focus as she did a mental inventory of the supply she had on hand, she being the kind of person who keeps ginger, fresh and crystallized, in her well-stocked kitchen. She probably also has a pound cake pan, if there is such a thing.

"A lot. Plus a boatload of bittersweet chocolate and a ton of ground almonds."

"Well, if that's the way you measure, it's no wonder you can't cook." She started to reach for the magazine, but stopped. "No. I haven't got time." Marshalling her strength, she pulled her gaze from the magazine and marched toward me. "Don't look so disappointed, Margaret," she flapped a hand back at the *Gourmet*. "I've got something much better for us to do and you don't need the pounds from that pound cake, anyway."

I ignored her crack about my extra padding and concentrated, instead, on the pronoun.

"Us?"

"It'll be fun." The fat manila envelope she pulled from under her arm and the day-glo glint in her eye made me nervous. "Look at these," she said, spilling the envelope's contents across the counter.

She'd brought several dozen photographs. Some were obviously copies of old snapshots and postcards showing Stonewall a hundred or so years ago. I'd seen most of them, or ones like them, in *A Pictorial History of Stonewall*, a perennial hotcake about our sleepy Tennessee town.

The rest of the pictures were much more recent and they were brilliant, both in color and execution. They showed details of doors, windows, porch railings, brickwork. There were streetscapes shot from unusual vantage points and candids of people I recognized.

"When were these taken?" I asked, holding up one that caught a couple of the old guys who doze on the sunny benches around the courthouse.

"Yesterday. Aren't they great?"

"They actually make Stonewall look interesting and possibly intelligent. And warm without being cute and fuzzy. Or sweaty."

"It's the light."

"Thanks for showing them to me." I picked up one with red geraniums massed in planters along the curb in front of a Federal Era building. "The city does a nice job with these geraniums downtown. Is this Idella's place? Wouldn't you love to live in a house like this?"

"It's got permanent rising damp."

"You can hardly see it in the picture."

"We can't use that one anyway, though." Bitsy took it from me, holding it with two fingers by the corner as though the rising damp might spread. "Idella would have a conniption. See? You can just make it out in the window on the left."

"Make out what?"

"Her cyclamen is drooping." Bitsy's face registered the horror apparently appropriate to this bombshell. Mine must not have.

"It's a plant, Margaret."

"Oh, right. Well, here's another one you can't use." I fished it out from under a shot of the post office. It was George Buckles, leaning against his squad car, toasting the photographer with a cup of coffee. "This one is unrealistic. The rest are wonderful, though. So why *are* you showing them to me?"

"Guess who's on the new Town Economic Promotions and Image Development committee?"

"You? That's great, Bitsy. You'll be an asset to the committee."

"Not just me, us! And we'll be so good at it!" She started bouncing on the toes of her spotless, white sneakers, showing the extent of her excitement.

"Tepid."

She stopped mid-bounce. "You haven't even heard what it's about, yet, Margaret. It doesn't help to start a new project with a poor attitude. You, of all people, being a business person, should know that."

"Not me, Bitsy. Town Economic Promotions and Image Development. T.E.P.I.D. Didn't anyone notice?"

"Typical," she said. "The first order of business will be to get the name changed. The second is a full-color, tri-fold brochure."

"Then I think you've got two different brochures going on here." I pushed the yellowed black and whites into one pile and the color shots into another. "So what's your focus? Who're you marketing to?"

"See? I knew we'd be good at this."

"What's with the 'us' and 'we,' Bitsy?" I went around behind my sales counter, a nonverbal cue I hoped she'd interpret as 'Busy. Not interested.' I picked up my stock replenishment report and put a pencil behind my ear for good measure. "You didn't really sign me up for this committee, did you?"

"You won't need to come to any of the meetings. Huh, you're right about this picture of George. It's wrong, somehow, but I can't think why."

"He never smiles with all his teeth like that."

"Hm," she said, not really paying attention. She was caught up in moving the pictures around in various arrangements so I took the pencil from behind my ear and added sound to my visual cue by tapping it on the countertop.

"Isn't that funny?" she said without looking up. "I find myself tapping a pencil against my teeth when I'm thinking. We're more alike than you like to admit."

The bell over my door rang, saving me from admitting anything.

"Hi, George."

"'Lo, Margaret."

"Let me see you smile, George."

"Don't start, Margaret. Not in the mood."

"Oky doke."

"Still living with your mother, George?" Bitsy asked.

George stopped and gusted a sigh in Bitsy's direction, his doggy brown eyes showing the depth of his pain at having to admit his living arrangements. Then he slumped off into the used book room, probably headed for the philosophy section. George is a nihilist. Or maybe an existentialist, I forget which. Whatever else he is, he's a depressed policeman.

"Touchy subject, there, Bitsy."

"You shouldn't have dumped him, Margaret."

"We dated for three months fifteen years ago and it was a mutual parting. You'll notice we're still friends."

"Anyway," she said, "he's worth ten of what's-his-name. Speaking of whom," she peered around in an exaggerated way, "isn't he somewhat conspicuous by his absence?" Ah, that's what this project was all about. Gene, the occasional man of my dreams, had been gone for several weeks and Bitsy was offering me useful activity as a diversion, bless her well-pressed heart. Her solicitude was especially touching because she doesn't like Gene. Unfortunately, I and my rumpled heart are not so easily touched.

"Why don't you do the brochure yourself, Bitsy? You were the cheerleader in high school and you know I've never been into boosterism."

"But, Margaret, you're the one who owns a bookstore."

"That only means I have a business license and probably know how to read. Not that I'm any good at or want to write tourist propaganda."

"I remember a very persuasive letter to the editor detailing how the train depot could be turned into studios and office space for the Arts Council." Her nostrils flared at the memory of that skirmish in the war between history and progress in Stonewall. Then she turned pensive as something else occurred to her. "If you'd worn that sweet jacket and skirt I gave you, when you spoke before the Board of Mayor and Aldermen, they might have taken that suggestion more seriously."

"I hope the decision to tear down the train station wasn't based on my fashion faux pas."

"The point is, Margaret, you have good ideas and you tried."

"How about this, then, 'The town of Stonewall is old. Local youth say it snores somewhere near the mountains on the east side of Tennessee. The population has never quite made it to 50,000 even when summer residents and tourists are conspicuous.' What do you think?"

"You are so negative."

"More like realistic, Bitsy. A brochure like this should be written by someone who knows what they're doing and is enthusiastic about it." I shrugged. "I'm not either one."

"No, I guess you're not. About the only thing you're enthusiastic about these days is wallowing in your own self-pity because what's-his-name left town. I can also see that my efforts to involve you in something other than your own misery are unappreciated and unwanted." She started gathering the photographs.

"Wait." The corner of something familiar and dear to me caught my eye. How had I missed seeing this one? I cradled it in my hands, taking in the lines of the porch roof, the bricks mellow in the late afternoon sun, the eccentrically uneven steps leading to the front door... "Wow."

"You should sand the door and repaint it. But I agree," Bitsy added after a quick glance at my face, "the place looks terrific. It's probably the best picture I've ever seen of the shop."

Something about the gloat in her eye, so nearly approaching a smirk, tempted me to remain adamant with my 'no'. But those pictures and what they did for Stonewall... I looked again at the photograph of my house, where my livelihood takes up most of the downstairs and I take up some of the upstairs.

"Okay," I said, "I'll help with the brochure. But on one condition."

"I'll make sure you get you a copy of that picture. An enlargement, even."

"Two conditions then. I also want you to make a really nice dinner. Soup or salad to start, something French for a main course, and that ginger chocolate pound cake from *Gourmet* for dessert. Drop it all off tomorrow night at seven-thirty and then disappear."

Bitsy glanced to the used book room and back. "Julia Child for two?"

"Yes."

"Deal."

"By the way, I'm delivering books to Idella after I close up this evening. Am I authorized by T.E.P.I.D. to tell her to water the whatsit in her window or remove it from sight?"

"No need for you to go all commando, Margaret. I'll come with you and tell her myself."

"Well, hell," I said, but only after the screen door had banged behind her.

"You moping, Margaret?" George, in his stealthy policeman shoes, caught me staring out the window.

"Hm?"

"Mashburn being out of the picture, and all."

"Gene's not out of the picture, George. He's in Paducah."

"That's not the same thing?"

"He'll be back. He's there working on the final drawings for a rehab of some river warehouses."

"So, why does Bitsy think he's gone for good?"

"She has her hopes and dreams."

"And you two enjoy aggravating each other." George shook his head. "Not necessarily a healthy hobby."

"Probably not. Habits do die hard, though. Did you find anything good back there today? Philosophy? Theology?"

He held up a used copy of Kafka's *Metamorphosis*.

"Heard it's a hoot. You know, Margaret," he leaned in, looking alarmingly fatherly, "it wouldn't hurt you to lighten up. Find a better hobby. New vistas. You know?" Free mental health tips from the neighborhood Nietzsche who still lives with his mother. He nodded, paid, and plodded back out the door.

Delivering books isn't part of my normal business routine, but I do it for some of my elderly and shut-in customers. And though George might not recognize "collecting" old ladies as a hobby, it does occasionally open enticing new vistas. I've spotted early Agatha Christie first editions living with a frail widow in a ranch house on Walnut Street and Idella Humphries allows me supervised visits with her 1940 copy of *the lives and times of archy and Mehitabel* inscribed by Don Marquis to 'Dearest Dell'. Idella and I aren't so chummy that *I* call her Dell, but I'm happy when she phones every few months with another book order.

Bitsy and I arranged to meet at Idella's at seven. I stepped out the door, after a satisfying day of bookselling, into a fine, late summer evening. Cicadas revved overhead and the purple asters were starting their annual race of color around my yard and down the back alleyway. Deciding my car with its indigestion would be an intrusion, I left the wildlife to its riot and strolled the eight blocks from my end of Main Street to Idella's.

Stonewall is a great town for walking even though, like some of its inhabitants, it struggles with its identity. On Main and adjacent streets there are enough Victorian houses with their deep front yards and Federal Era buildings hugging the sidewalks to give us the vaguely 'lost in time feel' that draws tourists. Houses like mine, from the 1920s and 30s, lend another style of quaint to the scene and the smattering of post-war frame houses manages to hold their own. The whole architectural mishmash gives the place a lived-in, slightly untidy, look that appeals to me. But I still avert my eyes when I pass the convenience store that replaced the train station.

A block and a half from Idella's I saw Bitsy and even from that distance I could tell she was agitated. Something about the tight circles she was walking in and the way she kept looking at her watch. Call me perverse, but I slowed down. When she saw me, she interrupted her pacing and started toward me.

"When did you talk to Idella?" she barked from a block away.

Over and around the First Methodist steeple, swallows were looping after insects in the twilit sky. I watched them, enjoying the calm in my immediate vicinity. Were they swallows? Maybe they were bats. Bitsy jogged the last half block between us.

"Oh, hi, Bitsy. Isn't it a lovely evening?"

"Did you talk to her today?"

"No, I talked to her last week when she ordered the books. I talked to her machine this morning and let her know the books were in and I'd drop them by this evening. That's S.O.P. with Idella. Why the swivet?"

"She didn't answer when I knocked."

"Don't worry about that, you just don't know the secret knock."

"Margaret, I'm not kidding."

"I'm not either. Idella's paranoid on top of being reclusive. She doesn't answer her phone and if you don't knock the right way she won't open the door."

"But Margaret…"

"Come on, I'll show you."

"Fine," she said, "but first I'll show *you*." She hustled me the rest of the way to Idella's, pulling to a stop in front of the window with the whatsit. "Look at the cyclamen, Margaret."

I looked and shrugged. It was droopier than in yesterday's photograph, but not much different from many of the houseplants I've had over the years. "You don't think it'll perk up if she waters it? You aren't really worried about her whatsit ruining your picture, are you?"

"No, Margaret, I'm worried about Idella. I might not know her secret knock, but I do know she'd never let her whatsit wilt."

I shifted my gaze from the plant to Bitsy. She looked back at me and there was very little of the fussy busybody in her eyes, now. Most of what they showed looked like genuine concern.

I nodded, stepped past her, and rapped 'shave and a haircut' on Idella's door. There was no quavering 'come in'. I knocked louder and peered through the sidelight, then stooped to retrieve the spare key.

"Under the mat? If she's so paranoid, why does she keep a key under the mat?"

"She's paranoid but old fashioned." I unlocked the door, knocking on it again as I swung it open. "Idella? Yoohoo, Idella. It's Margaret."

Bitsy followed me into the wide entryway. She bumped into me when I stopped, as I always do, to smile at Idella's amazing collection of mismatched bookcases and their eclectic contents. They start in the front hall, lining both walls, some reaching up to the ceiling, a few leaning companionably against their less tipsy neighbors, and they carry on through the doorways into Idella's other rooms, beckoning beguiled readers after them.

Bitsy bumped me again. "This is your kind of place, isn't it?" she whispered.

"Yes it is." I breathed deeply and sighed.

Bitsy sniffed. "I smell the rising damp."

"Shh," I said, "that's just old people smell." Then I called again, "Idella? Knock knock, it's Margaret." I ducked my head into the sitting room on the right, but no Idella, so crossed the hall to the twin sitting room on the left. "I've brought your books, Idella. Idella? *Idella?*"

She lay crumpled on the floor and didn't look as though she'd be perking up any sooner than her cyclamen. I tried, anyway, feeling for a pulse at her throat, her wrist. There was nothing. She was cold. And when I finally caught my breath I knew she'd probably been that way for a while.

"Don't touch the phone," Bitsy said as I started toward it.

"We need to call someone."

"There might be fingerprints."

"It's not a crime scene, Bitsy."

"You don't know that."

I looked around at the shelves, the books, Idella's shabby old overstuffed chair. They seemed frozen, as though in shock.

"Watch this," Bitsy said, snapping me back. "Rodney bought me this for emergencies." She pulled a cell phone from her purse and pressed some buttons. "Huh. Why didn't that work? I programmed it so all I have to do is this," she pressed the sequence again, "and I'm supposed to get 911."

"Why don't you just dial 911?"

"This is supposed to be faster."

"But this is probably better." I took the phone from her and dialed George.

I was surprised by how thoroughly Bitsy and I fell apart when George arrived. He let us sit in the kitchen while he got on with his business and made more phone calls in the sitting room.

"You two need another box of Kleenex?" he asked, hovering in the doorway a little later.

"We're okay, George. Thanks. Is she, have they..."

"Yeah. Just left with her."

I blew my nose.

"Wasn't anything you could do, Margaret. They're guessing she passed sometime yesterday, maybe even the day before." George shifted his feet. "Um, Margaret, do you mind coming with me? Look at something?"

In the space I hesitated before answering, Bitsy reanimated.

"Oh my god I knew it she was murdered. Someone broke in and hit her over the head. Margaret, don't go with him. Get a lawyer. I'll get a lawyer. I'll call one right now..." She jumped up, but before I could react, George was there, hands on her shoulders, steadying her.

"Bitsy, you're babbling," he said. "No one's said anything about murder."

"But…"

"I just want to ask her a few questions about, um, er, about some of Idella's books. No need for you to even stay. You can go on home."

"I'm not leaving without Margaret." Bitsy, in all her five-foot-two glory, was ready for battle.

"I'll be fine." I gave her a hug, which surprised us both. Then I thought of something that might make us both feel better. "I always made a pot of tea for Idella when I came by, George. Would it be okay if Bitsy makes one, now? It'd be kind of nice, like saying goodbye. The tea's in that cupboard and the kettle's on the stove."

He nodded. "This time of day, though, you should see if there's any herbal or decaffeinated."

From the look on her face and the fists on her hips, Bitsy wasn't entirely convinced I didn't need her charging forth on my behalf. Either that or she didn't appreciate George telling her how to choose an appropriate evening beverage. Whatever the reason, when he turned to leave the room, she performed a surreptitious bit of complicated semaphore. Then, smiling grimly, she shooed me after him and started filling the kettle.

"So what books do you want me to look at?" I asked George, wondering what in the world Bitsy thought she'd just communicated to me.

He answered with a grunt about as decipherable as Bitsy's mime.

"At least tell me what I'm looking for. And why. And is it really okay to go traipsing around like this? It *isn't* a crime scene, is it?"

"Fisher and I went through the whole place before they left with the body. I just want to look at a few things again. Get your opinion."

"On what?"

"In general."

"It's a little creepy, George."

"Nah, come on. We'll start up there."

I followed his broad back up the stairs, curious, despite the spider doing a Samba down my spine. As many times as I'd visited Idella, I'd never been upstairs. George gave another grunt when we reached the top landing, but this time I knew exactly what he meant.

It turned out Idella's passion for books carried on upstairs with the same fervor as down. But where the bookcases downstairs maintained at least a degree of decorum, these shelves in the upper hall were a drunken revelry. There were books on every available surface, books in stacks, stacks forming pyramids. Glancing up, I half hoped to see books swinging from the chandelier.

"What do you see, Margaret?"

"Ah, George, I see wonderful things. I'm going to miss Idella. You know, though, there's no possible way I can tell you if any books are missing."

He went into one of the front bedrooms without answering. I hung back to trail a finger over spines and covet titles. I'd had no idea of the depth of Idella's obsession or the breadth of her collection. Mark Twain rubbed shoulders with Michael Crichton on one side and Stephen Hawking on the other. An algebra text and a dated electric code handbook mingled with a group of Harlequins. Shade gardening mixed with light poetry. And speaking of mixing, on top of a Seussian stack of picture books lay M.F.K. Fisher's translation of the brilliant French chef Brillat-Savarin's *Physiologie du Goût*. And it was cuddling with a biography of my hero, Julia Child. Feeling somewhat guilty for disturbing the party, I removed Julia from Brillat-Savarin's clutches and tucked her under my arm.

I heard George open a closet and move coat hangers along the pole. Then he opened and closed several windows.

"What are you looking for?" I asked when he brushed past me. "She had a stroke or a heart attack, didn't she?" I held onto Julia and followed him into the room opposite. He checked these windows, too. "You'd need a ladder to get in that way, wouldn't you?"

"Hm?"

"If you're thinking someone got in through a window. They're kind of high up. You'd need a ladder, right? Besides, that's Main Street. Wouldn't someone notice a…" I shivered, "anyone climbing in? Even at night? And anyone could find the key under the mat." I was babbling like Bitsy.

George brushed past me again and went to look in the bathroom, where I heard him mutter "Damn."

"What? What?"

"Been a while since I've seen anything like this. Take a look."

I didn't. I couldn't. I hugged Julia.

He stuck his head back out the door. "It's the tiles, Margaret. Some of them look hand-painted. What's the matter?"

Tiles? Julia almost came to my rescue by smacking him upside the head. Instead, we joined him in the bathroom.

"Linen closet's kind of poky," he said, closing it and opening the medicine cabinet. "But what do you think?"

"What do I think? I thought you'd found some sort of horrible evidence in here, George, what do you mean what do I think?"

George experienced an 'aha' moment worthy of any great detective. "Evidence? Oh, no, sorry. They'll do an autopsy, but you're right, it was probably her heart or a stroke. I mean what do you think about the house, Margaret? Do you realize how hard it is to get your hands on a place like this?"

"You're house-hunting?"

"Not to buy. Idella rented. No one else knows it's available, yet, except for those E.M.T.s, and Fisher. And Fisher found a place a couple months back when old Merv Ledford stroked out."

"George Buckles, I am appalled."

"Idella's gone, Margaret."

"Just barely."

"Someone's going to end up renting the place."

"And this is the time to look it over?"

"Why not?"

I stared at him.

His own eyes dropped to study his shoes then met mine again. "I'm a cop, Margaret. For me, a situation like this is a mundane moment."

"Not for me or Bitsy. Not for Idella."

He heaved a sigh not quite large enough to span the chasm between us. "You're right and I'm sorry I've added to your shock and grief. But that doesn't change things. You and Bitsy go on home. I'm going downstairs, find out who she paid rent to. Make a few phone calls."

I followed him, but halfway down sank onto a step.

"You feeling okay, Margaret?"

"Feeling surreal, George. I'm going to sit here a minute."

Bitsy found me there, reading about Julia's early days in Paris. "I see you've retreated," she said, handing me a cup of tea.

I held the cup and inhaled wisps of steam. "What do you mean?"

"You're reading." She sat down next to me. "Your nose in a book is like me in a kitchen. That worked, by the way, so thank you. Making the tea gave me a chance to pull myself together, otherwise I would have done exactly what I said."

"That bit of sign language? What was that?"

"I said I was going to call Rodney, then find Idella's frying pan and use it on George if he started accusing you of something. You didn't get that?"

"Sorry."

"It wasn't a good plan, anyway. I realized that while I made the tea. I also realized if there was anything suspicious about Idella's death, George wouldn't be the only policeman still poking around asking questions. So what *did* he want?"

"My opinion. He's thinking of renting the place."

"What? Oh my god." She stood up and looked around, aghast as only Bitsy can be. "That's so… Oh my god. Come on, Margaret, let's get out of here."

"Good idea."

I took the biography back to its party upstairs, then remembered the bag of books I'd brought for Idella and retrieved it from the kitchen. I stopped to let George know we were leaving. He was on the phone, smiling with all his teeth, and gave me a thumbs-up.

Bitsy gave me a ride home. We sat quietly for a minute after she pulled into the drive.

"Well, that was incredibly sad," she finally said. "Idella was a nice old lady."

"Was she?" I asked turning to look at her. "I was just thinking I probably knew some of her books better than I knew her. And what does that say about me?"

Bitsy kindly didn't answer.

"I read something I liked in the Julia Child biography back there. She used to say, 'Life itself is the proper binge.'"

"And what does that mean to you?"

"I'm still working on it." I opened the car door. "So I'll see you tomorrow at seven-thirty with the French dinner?"

"You're kidding. After the way he behaved at Idella's? Surely you're not still having George over?"

"Not George, Bitsy. Gene. He gets back from Paducah tomorrow night."

She thought about that, shaking her head to help the process. "Huh. Well, I never thought I'd be glad *he* was back in the picture."

"Goodnight, Bitsy. Oh, and when's the next T.E.P.I.D. meeting? I think I'll come along."

"Tuesday at seven." She drove off still shaking her head as though, far from ceasing, wonders were buzzing in her ears.

I let myself in, climbed the stairs, and dumped myself into my pajamas. Then I padded back down, and while milk heated in the microwave, hunted up a copy of the Julia Child biography in the used book room. I set it in the middle of the kitchen table with the copy of *Being There* Idella had ordered but hadn't had the chance to read. Moving around the kitchen, in my own non-culinary way, I accomplished a decent cup of cocoa, nonetheless, and sat down opposite Julia and her new companion, raising my mug to them.

"Bon appétit."

In this story I paired the annual education fair at my children's school with a couple of newspaper articles I've never been able to get out of my head.

Judging Others

My sister Bitsy asked me to do her a favor. Which, in the ordinary course of human events wouldn't be anything worth mentioning, except that favors for Bitsy have a way of turning into something more than a borrowed cup of sugar or a few otherwise idle hours on a Saturday morning. Bitsy runs her life like a Swedish film. Every nuance of her day is fraught with symbolism and a chance for someone to screw up.

So you might wonder why I even considered saying yes. Maybe it's the full moon. Or something in the water. Probably it's just my natural *joie de vivre* egging me on, applauding behind my back every time I stand there looking into Bitsy's beady eyes and throw caution to the winds.

"Yeah, okay," I said. "I'll take over for Rodney. Why was he judging the short story contest anyway?" We were sitting in my living room, Bitsy prim in her pressed slacks and twinset, me on the arm of the sofa because the sofa itself was covered with books.

"Rodney's been writing poetry for years," said Bitsy brushing invisible crumbs from her lap.

"Rodney?" I asked, forgetting to cover my astonishment with tact. "Why?"

"Margaret, for someone who professes to know so much about good literature, you have an extremely narrow soul."

How could I argue with that? I wasn't even sure what it meant. But if it meant me not being able to picture Bitsy's husband, the rotund insurance salesman, dallying with sweet verse I guess she was right.

"Oh," I said, to cover my failing. "Well, leave the stories and I'll do what I can." I eyed the stack she dropped onto the one clear corner of the coffee table, calculating inches per evening. "When do you need them back?"

"You can keep them and give them back to the students when you hand out the prizes at the Education Fair."

"I have to hand out the prizes? You didn't say anything about that." Typical.

"For heaven's sake, Margaret. It's a small thing."

"Then why don't you do it?"

"As president of the Garden Club," Bitsy said, her voice swelling as she invoked the majesty of her newly won office, "I'll be judging the house plants."

"Oh." A word I find useful for many occasions with Bitsy. "When is the Education Fair?"

"Saturday morning."

I was silent for a minute while she avoided looking at me.

"Bitsy," I said then, because I believe in being honest, "this is Thursday."

"Thank you for reminding me, Margaret. I have a hair appointment. Goodbye!" And she fled, with my *joie de vivre*. I turned my back on the innocent stories and stalked out to the kitchen, regret pursuing me like a pack of dogs, and poured myself a cup of strong coffee.

"Hell," I said, burning my mouth on the first gulp.

"You forgot the 'o.' 'Hello' is a friendlier greeting." My sometimes dear one, Gene, came in the back door.

"Hi. Bitsy just got out the front door before I could strangle her."

"Well, that explains everything." He smooched me lovingly, having tracked bits of grass clippings across the floor to do so. "Including why I came in the back door. Did you hear about Jefferson Ice?"

"Bitsy told me in ten-inch headlines: JEFFERSON ICE AND COLD STORAGE DEFROSTED!" I do a fair imitation of Bitsy's high-pitched exclamations, even when not provoked. Gene gets a kick out of that because he's so often a target for the originals.

"Bitsy's taking it personally. Rodney's in charge of processing all the claims and has been at it day and night all morning. According to Bitsy, the amount and variety of stuff kept in cold storage is staggering. So now Rodney can't judge the short stories for the Education Fair, which if you ask me he should have finished by now anyway. So Bitsy asked me to do it." I mumbled that last sentence as I turned to rummage in a cupboard.

"What?" Gene asked.

I didn't repeat myself. Complaining about Bitsy loses its legitimacy when one is discovered aiding and abetting her. I changed the subject.

"Did you know that Rodney writes poetry?" I asked.

Gene looked thoughtful. "Hmm. Have you ever read one of his insurance reports?"

"Are you serious?"

"You don't think it's possible for a poetic soul to lurk inside those sans-a-belts?" he asked, obviously giving the idea some consideration.

"You must be out of your mind," I said, and started to elaborate but then Cousin Leona showed up at the back door.

"Good morning, Margaret," she said to me. "Good morning, dear," she said to Gene. "Margaret, you would look prettier if you smiled more often. I came by to let you know I'll be out this morning. I didn't want you to worry if you came over to borrow a tea bag and didn't find me." Cousin Leona is seventy-eight and worries that if she doesn't answer when I ring her doorbell I'll panic and break down the door. It's an antique door.

"You probably won't see me for a few days anyway, Cousin Leona," I said.

"Oh?" She looked slyly from Gene to me. She has a romantic streak.

"No, Leona," I said. "It's paper work. I've got a lot to catch up on."

"Bitsy suckered you into judging the short story contest, did she?" She's also smug because she knows everything.

"Would you like to help?" I asked, spreading my most winning smile across my face.

"No." She patted Gene's cheek and left.

Gene patted my cheek and poured himself a cup of coffee.

"Why don't you judge the stories the way my seventh grade grammar teacher used to grade papers?" He asked. "Take the whole stack, stand at the top of the stairs, throw the stories up in the air, and the one landing in the middle of the bottom step wins."

"That's an idea."

"It's how I make all my really tough decisions."

"How comforting for the people living and working in the buildings you design." I sidled up to him and beguilingly lost myself in his deep blue eyes. "So, what are you doing tonight?" I murmured.

"Mmm," he said, putting down his coffee cup, the better to answer, "Got anything particular in mind?"

"How about something with a literary theme?"

The sparkle dimmed as his eyes narrowed. One of the reasons I like the guy, he's so charmingly resistant to bull.

Well, a solo evening reading stories couldn't be any worse than starting the morning with Bitsy at the door.

Judging Others

Business that day was slow. Gene left for his office. I put the open sign on the front door. And it started to rain. Selling used and rare books out of my house has its advantages. Not having to get out in lousy weather is one. But lousy weather also encourages people to curl up with a good book in their own house, not brave the deluge to buy one from me. Between the bedraggled customers who did wash up to my door I thought of epithets for poetic insurance men and their wives.

Some of my best business comes and goes through the mail. I've never met Bertie Lambert, for instance, and don't even know if it's she or he. Bertie lives in Pioneer, Tennessee, which I can't find on a map. I've never figured out how s/he found me, but we keep up a mutually beneficial correspondence. Half the time I can't locate what Bertie is looking for. Sometimes I do and then I eat out for a week and put something aside for my late middle age. There's money somewhere in Pioneer. A letter from Bertie floated in with the day's mail. Bertie was looking for an Oscar Wilde first edition. Give me a break, Bertie.

Bertie's letter was the high point of the morning and things declined from there. Pretty soon reading short story entries looked exciting. I forced myself away from the bills that needed paying and picked the first story off the top of the stack, *'Death Rush to Alpha Centauri'*.

In 3,600 words I lived through an invasion, a plague, a near suicidal star cruiser flight, a torrid love affair, a jilting, a comeuppance, and a tidy finish. Plus an abridged dictionary of Star Speak. I might not live through a sequel but I was impressed. The author was in the sixth grade.

Then a polyester-type dripped through the front door and bought two Kitty Kelley hardback invectives. My least favorite kind of customer mating with my least favorite kind of book. Too bad I couldn't activate a small thermo-nuclear device hidden inside the cover the way Ras Sputum did in *'Death Rush to Alpha Centauri'*. Instead I accepted cash and picked up the next entry, *'Amazon Trails'*.

In 2,300 words I lived through an invasion, a plague, a near suicidal canoe trip, a torrid love affair, a jilting, a reconciliation, and a tragic ending. Probably true.

The rest of the afternoon I only absently attended to business, which was mostly absent anyway. To put a positive spin on it, there were enough stories to entertain me well into the evening, get me up bright and early Friday morning and enliven another whole day. More realistically, *'Licorice for Brittany Lynn'* gave me nightmares and several others, including *'Sam Gumbadum and the Magic Unicorn Horn,'* put me off my Grape Nuts. But mostly I enjoyed myself. Pathetic poetic Rodney didn't know what he'd missed.

The problem came in picking the winners. Gene's stair method had its appeal. So quick and decisive. Instead I diddled around coming up with ways to judge the stories, at one point going so far as to make a pile of the ones with misspelled words and another of those with blatantly poor grammar. I stood back to admire the results and was immediately horrified. Shuddering at the Bitsyish implications of those neat stacks, I shuffled everything back together again. After a few more lame ideas I finally just picked the three I liked best.

Piece of cake. I actually looked forward to patting the little pen wipers on their heads.

Friday evening Bitsy called to ask how it was going.

"How is what going?" I asked, getting in a quick, clean, cheap shot.

"Margaret!" Too cheap, I guess.

"All done, Bitsy."

"Well, that wasn't so bad, was it? Now don't forget tomorrow morning! Oh, and Rodney thought it would be nice to have you over for a barbecue tomorrow night to thank you. And what's-his-name." Bitsy goes out of her way to forget Gene's name. She has faithfully disapproved of him for three years now.

"Thanks. I'll tell what's-his-name."

She trilled a little and hung up.

Judging Others

I made a few unflattering remarks to the phone and sat down with the newspaper. Two articles caught my eye. In Texas a maniacal mother tried to strangle her daughter's rival on the cheerleading squad. And in Massachusetts a maniacal high school senior eliminated his rival for class valedictorian. Visions of getting up in front of rabid parents and insane children churned through my head. Then a vision of Bitsy, aggrieved, swarmed in. It was a tossup for ugly. I thought of calling Gene so that he could come hold my hand through the long night. But only his answering machine was home. I extended Bitsy's barbecue invitation to it and hung up. I didn't sleep well.

Saturday morning I dressed soberly, the idea being that a person who looks in charge is in charge. I wanted every advantage while facing a crowd of potential neurotics.

The Education Fair happens every spring. It's like one giant town-wide open house showcasing the best of the school year from the kindergartens through twelfth grade. As a child I'd looked forward to the fair. One year Bitsy tripped while crossing the stage. Another year our brother Mac won a prize for a report called "*Newts Are Our Neighbors.*" I think maybe I won something for a model of a wickiup. But I wasn't sure how things and especially the blood lust for competition might have changed during the intervening years.

I went to the fair early so there would be time to get a feel for the mood of the mob. Except for a few children looking dismal because their parents had them dressed like junior prom royalty, people looked happy and sensible. Good. I caught sight of Bitsy in her garden club regalia hovering in the distance, waved to let her see I was there, and headed in the opposite direction. There's something about Bitsy in a flowered hat that puts me off. And I know there's something about me in a mood that sets her off. Better to amble down the aisles of tables and look at the displays.

My favorite was a Rube Goldberg contraption put together by a seventh-grade girl. It involved dominoes, ramps, marbles, a racing car, several springs, levers, string, and a balloon in some complicated ways. The end result was that a light switch turned on. I was marveling over this when a familiar monosyllable at my shoulder made me jump.

"Hmph."

I turned to find Cousin Leona standing beside me which was unfortunate because in turning I knocked over several dominoes prematurely, sending the chain reaction in the wrong direction, earning me an acid glare from the seventh-grader. Not waiting for the words getting ready to boil through her father's teeth, I apologized, grabbed Leona by the elbow and hurried on to the next exhibit.

"Margaret, you should learn to relax," Leona said. Cousin Leona is above all else a retired teacher. She has endless energy to educate and improve the lives of those around her. Bitsy, in her middle age, is beginning to sound like our elderly cousin. But for some reason I don't mind Leona's pronouncements the way I do Bitsy's. Maybe it's the way they're meant. While Cousin Leona offers assessments with hope for improvement, Bitsy pinpoints failures. Cousin Leona means well. Bitsy is just unhappy.

I took two pieces of pizza being offered by a munchkin in a chef's hat and gave one to Leona. We relaxed happily, eating and wandering past handwriting samples and computer demonstrations and tables covered with sprouting beans and bubbling fluorescent beakers.

"Here's just what you need, Margaret." Leona stopped in front of a display titled "*Better Living with Herbs*." One of the boys behind the table was pouring something steaming into cups.

"Herb tea. It's got things in it that will pull you together." She took a cup for herself and handed one to me. Then, spotting one of her retired teacher cronies, she patted my arm and marched off. I headed toward the other end of the gym where the prizes were going to be awarded.

Judging Others

According to the program the short story prizes would follow a violin and flute duet. The schedule blithely left out what time that should be, but armed with Leona's calming brew, I only smiled. Just holding the warm cup was having an effect. So I stood around below the stage admiring the plants decoratively placed along its edge, listening for the strains of flute and fiddle.

The pizza had been good, but surprising, because of an entire fleet of anchovies cruising beneath the cheese. Now Leona's tea could happily serve two purposes. Judging it cool enough, I brought it toward my lips. The cup didn't get beyond three inches short of my nose. Health-giving, peace-loving herbs they might once have been, but the smell of that concoction was incredible. It was absolutely repulsive.

I didn't quite feel like retching, so maybe the ingredients did have some value, but I did the next best thing. To the final notes of the duet on stage, I dumped the stuff surreptitiously into one of the plants. Feeling pleased at such a quick, calm reaction, silently thanking Leona for that much at least, I tranquilly climbed the steps to announce the short story prizes.

Amazingly enough, no one said boo about the prizes. Parents beamed. I beamed. The winners blushed becomingly. Patting the author of *'Death Rush to Alpha Centauri'* on the head turned out to be inappropriate as he was several inches taller than I am. The photographer from the local paper took pictures. The applause made me feel wise in my decisions. My faith in the goodness of my hometown and the sanity of its parents and children was restored.

I even beamed at Bitsy in her flowered hat as I left the stage. Then I went in search of a large, cold, non-herbal drink and some lunch.

So what is it about fate or destiny that can't leave one person alone?

I went back to the gym after a sustaining quantity of cafeteria carbohydrates and there was Bitsy in the middle of the stage being accosted by a woman brandishing a sick looking houseplant.

"It was sabotage!" the woman was hissing at Bitsy. "Someone poisoned it."

Bitsy quite often irritates the hell out of me. Usually I just let her. We're sisters. But I don't like seeing other people treating her as I'd sometimes like to.

"Bitsy, can I help?" I asked, coming up behind them.

The woman with the plant turned, now cradling it, and pushed a snuffling child to the fore.

"Angela's plant," she said, "deserved first prize for philodendrons and this woman gave the prize to Brittany Daniels." She gestured first at Bitsy and then to a small girl standing defiantly next to a robust plant.

"There doesn't really seem to be much comparison," I said.

"Not now there isn't!" Angela's mother spat. "That Daniels girl poisoned Angie's!" On cue, Angie started crying. So did Brittany Daniels. Then Mrs. Daniels erupted on the scene.

I was still feeling the effects of my stint as wise and well-loved short story judge and thought maybe I could show the people in Massachusetts and Texas how saner people do things. I motioned to Bitsy who looked ready to curl up and die herself. Together we steered the battle towards the gap in the stage curtain and safely through it, out of the limelight.

"Now, let's all try to relax," I said. Angie hiccuped. Her mother growled deep in her throat. Mrs. Daniels smoothed her hair and made an effort.

"To my mind a plant can't win first prize if it's as limp as cooked spinach," she said.

"A plant can't win first prize if it's poisoned!" Angie's mother roared.

"My girl never touched your plant."

"Then you probably did it yourself!"

Where was Ras Sputum with his thermo-nuclear device when I needed him?

"Hmph."

Cousin Leona. The long arm of the iron-haired spinster teacher.

We all stepped back and sucked in our collective breaths. Leona stumped forward, took Angie's drooping plant from her mother's grasp and held it next to one she'd brought with her. The plants looked like twins in distress, the second as bedraggled as the first.

"I think they should each receive a first prize," said Cousin Leona. "Posthumously."

"Urrgh," gargled Brittany and Mrs. Daniels upon realizing the second plant was theirs.

"What happened?" asked Bitsy, clutching the curtain for support.

"My god," said Angie's mother, "there must be someone after both our girls!"

With shocked faces the mothers gathered their daughters to them and together they hurried out, stage left, with furtive glances all around.

"This is terrible!" Bitsy shrilled.

I had to agree. "I thought the children and parents around here were different," I said shaking my head. "This really is disgusting."

"They're sick."

"Moral cretins," I said.

"Well," said Bitsy, adjusting both her hat and her mouth to a grim angle, "we'll just have to find out who did it."

"I did it," said Cousin Leona.

"What?" We stared at her.

"Only the second one. Margaret killed the first one." I continued to stare at Leona but Bitsy's eyes swiveled around to bore into me.

"Margaret!"

"She poisoned it with herbal drain cleaner," said Leona calmly.

"Margaret!"

Now my mouth was hanging open, something Leona tells me is unbecoming.

"Well, it was an accident, dear," Leona said. "I told her it was tea. I thought it was. I should be more observant. Anyway, when I went after Margaret to tell her not to drink it I saw her pour it into the plant."

"So why did you kill the other one?" Bitsy shrieked.

"I had to be sure, dear. I didn't want to accuse anyone falsely."

"Cousin Leona..." Bitsy started.

"They're waiting out front for the rest of the prizes," Cousin Leona cut in, giving Bitsy the benefit of her teacher's eye. Bitsy choked a bit then backed out through the curtains.

"Cousin Leona..." I began.

"Margaret, dear," she said, "next time don't be so quick to judge others." And she departed, stage right.

I followed her out feeling limpish and a bit deflated like the ex-philodendrons.

Bitsy was still on stage. From the color in her cheeks, and the regal gestures she was bestowing left and right, I could see that her spirits were reviving full bore. And from the look she blasted in my direction as I slunk away I figured the invitation for backyard barbecue was off.

So I went home and called Gene. He came over and we spent the evening reviving our own spirits.

*Available now from Darkhouse Books, "Wilder Rumors"
by Molly MacRae. Please enjoy this bonus chapter!*

Lawn Order

A Margaret & Bitsy Mystery

Molly MacRae

Chapter 1

The morning my sister Bitsy flung a dead pigeon on my bookstore sales counter was the morning I decided to redefine my mission in life.

"Margaret," she demanded, "just look at that."

I was trying not to, but it was hard to miss, splayed as it was, like a bad joke, between the cash register and a display of *Elegant and Economic Dinners for Two*. I grabbed a bag, swiped the bird into it before the customers browsing the shelves saw it, and gave the counter a quick, disinfecting spritz. Taking a closer look at Bitsy I could see she wasn't going to be as easy to get rid of. The light of the fanatic burned in her eyes.

"Bitsy, what's gotten into you?"

"There are hundreds of them out there around the courthouse."

"So you, what..." I asked, trying for a calming tone of voice, "...thought you'd do the town a favor and you shot one?"

"Don't be ridiculous." She leaned across the counter, beckoning me to do likewise. "It was poison."

"You poisoned it?" I recoiled, amazed. Reconciling this piece of news with the image I've always carried in my mind of Bitsy as the high priestess of the Latter Day June Cleaver Society wasn't going to be easy. How did this bit of toxic mania fit into the overall scheme of Bitsy as president of the Stonewall Garden Club, darling of the Stonewall Historical Society, happy alphabetizer of her medicine cabinet and linen closet? Actually, I don't know that she alphabetizes her linen closet, but she has that general air about her and if I turn around fast enough, sometimes, there's a look in her eye that makes me think she's itching to have a go at mine, too.

But the look on my face now betrayed my mind wandering down a road best not taken. I've never been good at hiding errant thoughts from Bitsy. Her high caliber voice snapped me back in line.

"Not me, Margaret. That swine."

"Shh, Bitsy." One of my customers was beginning to look interested in our conversation. He re-shelved the Wodehouse first edition he'd been drooling over for twenty minutes, moved closer, and took an unconvincing interest in the gazetteers at the end of the counter. "What swine?" I whispered, sliding down the counter in the opposite direction. I try to keep my business and my sister separate as much as possible for just this reason. A bookstore doesn't need to have the rarefied hush of a research library, but the din of a hyena's den gets on my nerves.

"That swine Douglas Everett," Bitsy failed to whisper back.

"Who?"

"You know very well who I mean."

"Well, yeah, Bitsy, of course I do. It's just that I'm dumbfounded. What did little Duckie Everett have against the pigeon?" I realized I was still holding the bag and handed it to her. She dropped it back on the counter.

"I don't want it. And for heaven's sake, Margaret," she said, brushing invisible pigeon specks from her blouse, "He's hardly 'little Duckie Everett' anymore. He's at least five years older than I am."

He's more like one year younger. Bitsy's cockeyed view of aging is grounded in some complicated formula involving mobiles, stabiles and tangential slopes. It's similar to the theory of continental drift, the central doctrine being her age is the only stabile and everyone else's flows on by. Someday I expect to be five years older than she is, too, though I started out two years younger. Fifty-three will try catching up to her next month, but she already has plans to be out of town so she can avoid it.

"Bitsy, I sense there's more to this story than a dead pigeon. Why don't you go on back to the kitchen and make some tea. I'll take care of these customers and join you in a couple of minutes."

She stalked off in that direction and I sighed with relief. I do love my sister, but she can't carry on a conversation in anything but Italics laced with exclamation points. Making tea has a soothing effect on her, though. Bitsy is one of those people for whom kitchen puttering is a tranquilizer.

In fact, I thought, as I rang up a magazine for one customer and the Wodehouse for the other, with that bit of inspired problem solving I'd killed two birds with one stone. But, as it turns out, that was an unfortunate turn of phrase to be thinking much less chuckling over. Too late, I remembered I hadn't done this morning's breakfast dishes, or any of yesterday's either.

"Oh, Margaret, really!" pierced the barrier of the kitchen door leaving all eardrums in its path quivering.

I sighed for a different reason this time, and after ringing up the last sale, I flipped the "welcome" sign on the door to its "back soon" side and went to join Bitsy in her idea of a domestic Superfund site.

The kitchen is the only part of my downstairs I keep private. I'm lucky enough to have what so many people dream of, a combination new and used bookstore in a great old house. Even better, Blue Plum Books and I live on tree-lined Main Street in Stonewall, my picturesque home town, nestled in the foothills of the Tennessee Blue Ridge Mountains. That Stonewall's population manages to hover under whatever magic number would make it ripe for inundation by mega-merchants isn't bad, either.

The house my books and I share is a two story Craftsman foursquare built in 1913 with the style's characteristic shingle siding, rafters, brackets, and deep porch. The books take up most of the downstairs and I take up some of the upstairs. It's an arrangement that has customers leaning their elbows on the counter, looking moonstruck, and telling me this would be their idea of heaven. The reality is that living at work can be hell, but what the hell, it's mine and I like it.

I bought the house and business as a package deal after spending a fruitful and unhappy decade applying my MBA as an investment banker in Chicago. Those were bountiful years for the stock market, when moderate sums of money morphed into bulging nest eggs seemingly overnight. But banking and the windy Chicago winters left my heart cold. So on evenings and weekends I ignored bluechips and bonds and warmed myself in bookstores and even ended up taking an evening job in my favorite one on Michigan Avenue. When Bitsy called to say Charlie Frank wanted to sell Blue Plum, I clapped my hands and packed my portfolio. I'd missed the hills and hollows of east Tennessee. I'd even missed Bitsy. But it was books that thawed my soul and lured me home.

Charlie Frank was a little old gnome surrounded by his family of books. He'd owned the house with the shop forever and parted with them only at the insistence of his human children, who were themselves past retirement age. After reluctantly turning the keys and deed over to me, he was supposed to emigrate to Florida and move in with a daughter. Maybe he did, though maybe he eluded the daughter by slipping inside a conspiratorial book and is spending his retirement in a story with a more exciting ending.

I quite easily slipped into the house and business and we've suited each other for almost twenty years, now. That's not bad considering small independent bookstores have been on the endangered business list for about as long.

When I bought the place, Bitsy helped spruce it up, Charlie having spent more time chasing rare editions than repainting or deep cleaning. Bitsy was in her element, choosing paint colors (pleasing earthy greens and blues) and suggesting chintz for curtains (immediately vetoed.) She also encouraged me to make the kitchen a part of the store and display the cookbooks there. Sort of like exhibiting zoo animals in their natural habitats. It was an appealing idea, but more appealing, instead, was being able to sit at the kitchen table in my pajamas not worrying about customer relations versus doing the dishes. Breakfast in pajamas and a lack of dish-doing are two of the differences between Bitsy and me. Once past our wren-brown hair, blue eyes, and general lack of height, several more differences lie in wait. Chintz curtains, for instance.

To make up for rejecting her kitchen and cookbook idea, I turned Bitsy loose on the front porch. Charlie had enclosed it for more floor space and included lovely windows in the remodel. But then he proceeded to cover the windows with a ramshackle collection of tall bookcases, creating a dark entryway with a piecemeal look. Bitsy saw the possibilities, though, and convinced me to have new shelves built around the windows. Now the porch walls are lined with bookcases and there are window seats for geraniums and enrapt readers. There are also several low, free standing units with shelves on all four sides and space on their table-tops for displays. Bitsy suggested moving the gardening and craft books to the porch and I did.

Bitsy stood, now, in the middle of the kitchen, teacup artfully aloft in her right hand.

"There were so many of them, Margaret." Her moue, comprised of equal parts distaste, aggrievedness, and belligerence looked as though it had been professionally applied. I wasn't sure which was causing her present unhappiness, the hundreds of poisoned pigeons flapping and dying around the downtown square or the dozen or so dirty dishes lounging shamelessly on the counter behind her. She looked poised to flee if the pots in the sink made a sudden move in her direction. There wasn't much I was willing to do about the kitchen at the moment, though, so I tackled the pigeons.

"Why couldn't you just tell me about them without bringing one along as a visual aid, Bitsy?"

"What?" She was leveling a bent eye at a sticky saucer on the stove and had lost the thread of the conversation.

"Why did you bring me a dead pigeon?"

"It was still alive and suffering and you're closer than the vet since he made that stupid move out to the highway. Why do so many people think progress means paving over the countryside and throwing up metal buildings?" Now she had the thread of the conversation, but if she headed off any further in that direction it was going to unravel.

"But Bitsy, I don't know anything about dying birds."

"No, but you have all those books out there."

"Oh, right. I'll go check my Dead Pigeon section. I think I squeezed it in between Classics and Children's Picture Books."

"There's no need to be sarcastic, Margaret. You know very well you've got books on all kinds of things."

"The library has more and you passed it on your way here."

Her moue got a little mouier and her eyes reflected her further pain. Bitsy had a run-in with the librarians several years ago when they converted to an automated self-checkout system. I don't know for certain why she hasn't set foot inside the library since then, but it's either a self-inflicted banishment or something the librarians voted on and wrote into an official addendum to library policy.

"You're always bragging about the books you can find for people that no other bookstore seems to be able to. Like that book on glass wigwam boats you found for that woman and then bored us all to death with for weeks."

"It was *Glaswegian Shipbuilding: 1830-1920*. Out of print. Rare."

"Whatever. You found it and so I thought a small thing like help for a suffering pigeon would be something you could handle.

You've got the *Mayo Clinic Guide to Family Medicine* out there. Surely you have something along those lines for pets."

"Oh, but Bitsy, wild birds are different."

"And it's dead now, anyway, so what's the use." She dumped herself into a chair at the table and it was an indication of how upset she was that she didn't brush off the toast crumbs first.

"Has anyone called the street department or whoever it is who picks up dead animals?"

"Who knows?" Bitsy does despondent almost as well as she does aggrieved.

"Someone probably already has by now but maybe you should call anyway to make sure. So then, uh, how exactly do you know Doug poisoned them?"

"Well, they aren't like lemmings, Margaret. They didn't all just take it into their heads to jump off the courthouse without flapping their wings."

"I mean, how do you know Doug is responsible? That's kind of hard to believe."

"Isn't it obvious?"

The only thing obvious to me was that talking Bitsy through this crisis was going to take longer than I'd expected. Though why, I muttered to myself as I scrounged around for a clean cup, I should ever expect any crisis of Bitsy's to die a quick, clean death I don't know. Maybe it's my eternal optimism that keeps bubbling up. A bit of misplaced *joie de vivre*.

Bitsy made a face when I sat down across from her with my tea and took a sip. She hates my "Eat More Possum" mug. "It's obvious because he's a member of the Progress Through Paving Party," she sniffed.

"You know that isn't its name."

"It might as well be."

"And how does that tie in with poisoning pigeons?"

"Don't you see?" she asked, impatient with my denseness. "It's all part of the plan. Kill off business downtown so people will go out to those new places along the highway to shop."

"By killing off the pigeons?"

"Would you take your children downtown to shop if they were going to see pigeons dying on the sidewalks?"

"But, Bitsy, doesn't Doug own buildings downtown? Why would he sabotage his own businesses?"

"He thinks pigeons are a nuisance and hates the mess they make on his window ledges. He says they're like rats with wings."

"Rats are probably smarter. But Bitsy, first you said he was sabotaging downtown and now you're saying he's doing some sort of cockeyed community service project. Which is it? And how do you know it was him?"

"Anyone would know it was him."

"But do you have any proof? Did anyone see him sitting on a bench passing around poisoned popcorn?"

"Margaret, I assumed you would be on my side in this matter."

"What side, Bitsy? It was a gross and nasty thing to do but you don't really know who did it. Maybe it was the town, they've come up with dumber ideas. But if you've got proof it was Doug, go to the police. There's bound to be a law against wasting winged rats."

"Margaret. It is not a joke."

"No, you're right. I'm sorry. But you've got to be careful about assuming you know who did it and very careful about going around saying you know for a fact he did it."

She was very careful as she put her teacup on the table. "Douglas Everett and his buddies are not good for this town. I am not assuming this. I've heard enough reports from reliable sources to know this for a fact. You, Margaret, as a small business owner should be more aware of and certainly more concerned about what's going on. Things are changing in Stonewall and not necessarily for the better. But there are some of us who have our eyes on Mr. Everett and we will fight him. That's the side I assumed you would be on."

She gathered herself and her shrouds of glory and stood to leave. "And Margaret, I'll take the bag with the pigeon. I'm afraid if I left it here you might lose it amongst the dishes and not find it again until next month."

I usually let Bitsy have the last word in situations like this. It gets her out of my hair sooner. Besides, she knows how to make a good exit and why rob her of an opportunity?

Which brings me back to the redefinition of my mission in life as precipitated by Bitsy and her ex-bird. Oddly enough, almost any time I redefine it, Bitsy ends up getting a mention. I haven't analyzed this phenomenon and I'm not sure I ought to. Some mysteries are best left in their own dark corners.

Having a mission in life isn't something I spend a lot of time brooding over. But occasionally giving it definition seems to give my life a sense of direction. Or maybe it's just that it gives me a sense of control as I wallow along in the river of life. "Lock all doors and windows anytime you see Bitsy coming," for instance, gave me a wonderful feeling of empowerment for a short time last spring.

I was waxing nostalgic over that memory when the regrettably unlocked kitchen door opened. I jumped, sloshing tea across the table. But it wasn't Bitsy back to blight my day further. It was our elderly cousin Leona. She has an uncanny talent for slipping through the front door without jingling the bell.

"I didn't think that was your trouble, Margaret," she said, surveying the scene. She tottered over to the sink and unearthed a dishrag and handed it across to me.

"What? Being a slob?"

"No dear, that hasn't ever slowed you down. But you're not usually the nervous type. Why so jumpy?"

"Bitsy threw a dead pigeon at me this morning."

One of the reasons I like my late mother's cousin is she doesn't either ask me to explain statements like the one I'd just made or offer reproof. She confines her comments to monosyllables. They encapsulate volumes of accumulated observations of the Welch girls, which she's never lacked opportunities to collect. As children, Bitsy and I were in and out of Leona's house almost as much as our own several blocks away. Her ethnologic study really took wing, though, when I bought Blue Plum. Her house is conveniently next door.

"Hmph," she said, "your 'back soon' sign is on the front door."

"Oops."

I sent the dishrag on a half-hearted flight toward the sink and Leona followed me back out front. I flipped the sign on the door so that Tom Kitten was once again welcoming people to the bookstore.

"Have you been downtown yet this morning, Cousin Leona?"

"Yes, dear. I always walk down to Bertie's for a cup of coffee at eight o'clock. It makes me feel as though I'm getting a head start on the day. You should try it."

"Maybe I will sometime. Did you see anything unusual?" I stuck my head out the door and peered down the street toward the courthouse. My place is four blocks from downtown proper. The pigeons tend to hang out down there where they can catch up on courthouse gossip and panhandle on the square. There weren't any staggering in my direction.

"Like what, dear?"

"Like ..." I turned around to answer her, but instead of finding Leona of the comforting shirtwaist ready to give my worries perspective, I was surprised by a man I didn't know standing at the sales counter staring at me.

Read Molly MacRae's "Lawn Order" to find out what happens next!

Available now from Darkhouse Books, "Wilder Rumors" by Molly MacRae. Please enjoy this bonus chapter!

Wilder Rumors

A Lewis Wilder Mystery

Molly MacRae

Chapter 1

Lewis Wilder looked up from his bowl of chili and swore into his napkin as he wiped his mouth. Here came the third reason he wasn't going to be enjoying his meal. At least three was a number that gave the whole evening a sense of balance. It rounded out the general tone of disaster. Presented with a fourth reason, though, he might need to call it quits. He crumpled his napkin and dropped it on the table. He watched Paul Glaser get out of the sheriff's car he'd parked at the curb and head for the café door.

"Evening, Lewis."

"Paul."

Wilder didn't ask Glaser to join him. Glaser smiled and slipped into the booth opposite him anyway. Wilder pushed the bowl of chili aside and waited.

"Aren't you going to ask me what I'm doing here?" Glaser asked.

Wilder didn't answer, instead picked up his glass of iced tea and drank.

"Well, it ain't museum business," Glaser said, still smiling. "Or is it? Of course, you maybe already know this, but that fool who's calling himself the Fox hit a house out near Sycamore last night. Took the portable silver. Heirloom quality, according to the receipt he left. The guy's got a hell of an eye for good old stuff. Hell of a nerve, too. Real professional, every way you look at it. But, I gotta tell you, Lewis, he's got us running in circles. I'm about beat."

Wilder thought about suggesting Glaser spend more time on his treadmill or at the gym. He let his eyes linger too long on Glaser's paunch. When he met Glaser's eyes again the smile was gone.

"What, Paul?"

"He's been lucky so far."

"Not getting caught? Maybe he's smart."

"Smarter than me? Pshaw. More like full of himself. No, what I'm waiting for is the unexpected, which is something I always expect. Someone's going to walk in on him one of these times. And someone is going to get hurt. Or dead."

Wilder crushed a packet of crackers into the chili. He brushed the crumbs off his hands then met Glaser's eyes. "What do you want me to say, Paul?"

"Where were you last night?"

"Home."

"Alone?"

"As usual. What have you heard this time?"

"Same old."

Wilder ignored his stare and looked out the window onto Main Street. What a pleasant, sleepy little town this had seemed when he arrived six months ago. Virtually snoring. He glanced back at Glaser who looked close to snarling. He bowed his head and studied the oilcloth on the table, pushed cracker crumbs around with a finger. Then he shrugged, looked Glaser in the eye again, spread his hands, and gave his best insincere smile.

"I don't know anything about it, Paul."

"You say that every time."

"It's uncomplicated. I like that. I'm going to finish my supper now. I'll see you later."

Glaser slid back out of the booth, his stomach pulling the cloth cockeyed. He stifled a belch and left.

Wilder heard muffled giggles on the other side of the cafe. Swell, the second reason for this evening's indigestion reappearing for an encore. Two teen-aged girls popped out of their booth and blushed their way over.

"Hi, Mr. Wilder," one of them breathed.

"Was that the sheriff talking to you?" the other asked. Her eyes were alarmingly large and moony.

"Mmhmm."

"My mom doesn't think he should always be bothering you."

"Do I know you?" Wilder asked.

"Yeah. Well, no, but you gave our class a tour of the museum."

"Oh." Wilder decided not to eat out anymore except during school hours.

"Well, bye, Mr. Wilder. Bye."

They crowded through the door. He watched as they walked down the street, nudging each other in fits of giggles, heads together comparing notes and looking back to see if he was looking after them.

Being blushed over was one thing. Being admired because the sheriff considered him suspicious was something else entirely. And that made reason number four and time to head for the door himself. He passed his hand over his face and gave the back of his neck a hard rub.

"Hey, Lewis." A young woman touched his shoulder and slid into the booth. Wilder relaxed and gave her a genuine smile.

"Hey, Pam. I didn't see you in here."

"I was in the kitchen talking to my sister."

"Willie's your sister?"

"Has been all my life. Say, weren't those girls a little young for you?"

"I'm not sure, I think they might've been trying to set me up with their mothers."

She grinned and pushed a Styrofoam container across the table to him. "Here, Willie says yours is cold by now and you've hardly touched a bite. Take this home for later; have it after the board meeting."

"Oh hell, what time is it?"

"Better run."

"Thanks, Pam. See you in the morning." Wilder grabbed the container and a stack of folders from the seat next to him. "Tell Willie thanks." He fumbled with the door then jogged down the street wondering again why he'd thought this town and this job were such a good idea. As he passed a trash barrel he tossed the Styrofoam container into it. The number one reason for his indigestion was Willie's godawful chili.

"And what do you make of our mysterious good fortune, Lewis?" Dr. Edward Ramsey asked fifteen minutes later, as the 'new business' portion of the monthly meeting of the Nolichucky Jack History Museum's board of directors got underway. He leaned across the broad, boardroom table and raised one hairy gray eyebrow at Wilder.

Wilder considered scanning the faces of the other board members. It might be interesting to see how many of them showed more than casual interest in his answer. But Ed Ramsey was big on eye contact so he returned the look with his own serious gaze.

"As much use as I possibly can, Ed. There's an itemized list of recent expenditures in the monthly report you have in front of you."

"Thank you, Lewis," Ramsey said with a tight smile. "Next item…"

"Wait a minute, I'd like to catch up here." This from a usually absent businesswoman, Elaine Pagels. "Sorry, but what exactly is this good fortune you're referring to?"

"How can you not know that by now, Elaine?" This from Lillian Bowman, an always present and accounted for retired schoolteacher.

Wilder ducked his head and bit his cheek to keep from smiling too obviously. Elaine and several other board members, including Ed Ramsey, had survived fourth grade in Lillian's classroom. She still had the tyrant's moves down pat.

"It was in the minutes. If you read them, or at least paid attention, you would know."

"Elaine?" Ramsey asked.

"Oh, now, what'll it hurt to fill her in?" drawled Paul Glaser, sitting across from Wilder. "How about it, Lewis?"

"A waste of time," Lillian Bowman muttered.

"Go ahead, Lewis," Ramsey said.

"We've been receiving anonymous donations for the past several months," Wilder said.

"Money?"

"Yes."

"That's wonderful. No idea where it's coming from? How much, by the way?"

"Two hundred dollars," Glaser said, smiling like a shark. "Each and every month for the past four months. And, no, we don't know where it's coming from. Do we, Lewis? In fact I'd say the donor's a real sly fella."

"Even if Lewis knows who the donor is, Elaine," Ramsey said, addressing both his glare and his words to Glaser instead of Elaine, " he wouldn't tell us. The donor wishes to remain anonymous and I think Lewis has demonstrated that he can keep his mouth shut."

"Exactly my point, Ed, the boy's nothing if not good at keeping secrets."

Wilder groaned.

"Lay off, Paul," George Palmer murmured. He was sitting next to Glaser, running a finger around his clerical collar. It was a gesture Wilder had seen him make from time to time. Whether it was an unconscious habit or calculated he wasn't sure. It tended to have a quelling effect, though, even if accompanied, as now, by Glaser's snort. "The donations are a boon for the museum, Elaine. We're grateful and hope they continue. Shall we get back to current business?"

"Please," Lillian snapped.

"Report from the Acquisitions Committee," Ramsey said, and Lillian adjusted her glasses preparatory to summing up her committee's progress.

Wilder let Lillian's precise words march past him. She'd cornered him earlier in his office and given him the gist, including a rapturous description of a fern stand she'd located for the museum's Victorian Parlor. He glanced around at the other board members who were variously paying attention to Lillian or, in the case of Ramsey, Palmer, and Glaser, paying attention to him. Heckle, Jeckle, and Hyde. Not quite right for Ramsey and Palmer, but Glaser definitely had a streak of something running through him. Something Wilder didn't want to see closer up. As he caught Palmer's eye, Palmer winked at him. Wilder quirked the corner of his mouth in return. Nice to have a friend.

The rest of the meeting traveled the typed agenda without detour until the last item. This was a request Wilder had fielded from a CEO in California for information on the original Grindstaff Pepper Packing Plant. He'd found a photograph in the archives but hadn't been able to pinpoint the building's location out in the county.

"My father traded with Mr. Grindstaff. I know exactly where that plant stood," Lillian said, emphasizing each word with a peck of her pencil on the papers in front of her.

"Jake or Lloyd?" demanded Charlotte Reed, one of two board members older than Lillian, and so, immune to the remnants of her imperious classroom demeanor.

"What?"

"I said Jake or Lloyd. Because Jake was kin to the Grindstaffs of Watauga but never had anything to do with peppers. Tobacco.

That was Jake. And he ran a dairy herd. You just don't see dairy the way you used to anymore, do you? Except for Morris Ledford. He has a pretty little herd out there on the Holston. Holsteins on the Holston. That sounds like a title for a bovine romance novel, doesn't it? Now if you mean Lloyd, he was kin to the Grindstaffs of Little Limestone over there past the rock house and..."

And so the begetting of Grindstaffs and their farming particulars exhausted the remaining minutes of the meeting.

"Excuse me, Charlotte." At nine P.M. Ramsey stood up, his gathered papers already tucked under his arm. "Folks, I'll be out of town this Thursday through next. Back in time for the Pickers' Picnic. Lewis, any problems that come up that you can't handle probably aren't worth bothering any of these folks with, but if you must, let it be on your own head. Meeting adjourned."

Ramsey was a stickler for starting and ending meetings promptly and Wilder felt like kissing his hem every time he called a timely dismissal. He'd quickly learned how memories, both long and short, derailed any given meeting in Nolichucky. Before Ramsey became chairman, museum board meetings had been the worst by far. They'd often degenerated into contests of reminiscence with Wilder wondering when he'd get to see Lillian slug it out with some lesser mortal.

Chairs scraped the floor and those members speaking to each other started in on the first round of good nights. A simple good night was practically unheard of in Nolichucky. A gauntlet of good nights developed in most cases and Wilder was always on the lookout for shortcuts. He gathered his papers, now, and tried to look both relaxed and on his way somewhere else.

"You look pained, Lewis," Elaine Pagels said as he pushed his chair in. "Don't those donations make you happy? Lighten the load just a bit?"

"They're great, Elaine." He looked past her. Only Ed Ramsey between him and the door and Ramsey was building steam for his own escape. "Thanks for making it tonight," Wilder said, edging around her. "Will we see you next month?" Ramsey had cleared the door. Wilder looked back over his shoulder to catch Elaine's answer.

"Do my best. Good night."

"Night." Wilder turned and slammed into Paul Glaser.

"Good way to get whiplash, Lewis. Here, let me." Glaser stooped to help Wilder collect the file folders and papers that had ejected on impact.

"Lewis, are you all right?" Lillian tottered over.

Wilder took the papers Glaser was shuffling, jammed them into the folders, and stood up.

"Just clumsy, Lillian. I'm looking forward to seeing that fern stand. Good night." Wilder brushed past Glaser without meeting his eye and started for the door where Palmer intercepted him.

"Liar," Palmer whispered out of the side of his mouth as he waved goodbye to Lillian and Glaser. "You'll hate her fern stand."

"Damn right."

They made it through the door and clattered down the stairs of the county office building where the board meetings were held.

"Don't take Paul seriously, Lewis. I'm sure he doesn't take these rumors seriously. He's got an unfortunate sense of humor."

"Like stopping by the café to ask me for an alibi."

"He likes to needle you."

Wilder held the outside door for Palmer. Under the streetlight, he stopped and looked at him.

"What?" Palmer asked.

"Nothing. Goodnight, George." Wilder watched as Palmer headed toward his rectory at the east end of Main Street, then he turned and walked in the opposite direction.

Nighttime Nolichucky was washed in the soft glow of new reproduction Victorian gas streetlights, the latest effort in reinforcing the myth of a town lost in time and the foothills of the Blue Ridge Mountains. Wilder thought it would be nice if certain of Nolichucky's residents got lost. Starting with Paul Glaser.

He walked past the mixture of mostly Federal and Victorian era buildings and around a corner into a narrow drive between the Doak building and the old mercantile. He turned another corner into the unlit alley running behind Main Street. A network of these alleyways threaded between some and behind most of the buildings in town. Wilder liked the sepia tones of the gas lit streets at night, but he liked even better these shadow lanes behind the scenes. Here his footsteps echoed in the dark, a sound that hadn't changed over the last hundred years. He could pretend for the space of a few blocks that he'd been transported, maybe not to a simpler day, but at least away from some of the complications of this one. Tonight, home and a beer sounded good.

Wilder held the long-rifle loose, but ready across his knees. Twenty-five open-mouthed children, transfixed by his sinuous whisper, were rooted to the floor in front of him, the only movement in the room his mesmeric rocking.

"And just at sunrise, the widow Brown sees movement at the edge of the woods. There," he pointed and twenty-five heads turned to see the men he'd conjured out the window. "She sees them coming. The early light glints on the bridles of their horses, on the stirrups, on the rifles they carry. Tipton and his men are here to arrest John Sevier and take him to prison, over the mountains in North Carolina. The men approach the house, bridles jingling, leather creaking, horses snorting. The men are tired. They've been riding half the night searching for Sevier. You can see the weariness in their faces. All except Tipton's. Tipton's face is hard and he's looking for a fight.

"But Mrs. Brown sits in the doorway, rocking, just as she has all night. She is as solid in her chair as she is solid in her conviction. No one will take Nolichucky Jack without first getting past her.

"She watches them, now, as they draw closer. She rocks slowly, back and forth, back and forth."

The hypnotized children swayed in time to Wilder's rocking.

"Tipton and his men, still mounted, are in a semicircle, now, in front of the cabin. Everything is quiet. No birds sing, no crickets chirp. Even the horses have stopped whickering to each other. The only sound is the slow creak of the widow Brown rocking in the doorway with the long-rifle across her knees.

"Then Tipton bellows, 'Sevier!'"

The children jumped at Wilder's unexpected roar.

"'Sevier, you'll hang!' But there's no answer from the house," Wilder continued, reverting to his near-whisper. "So Tipton raises his rifle. The widow Brown's eyes follow his every move; they don't waver for even one second. Just as Tipton brings his rifle level, she jumps up." Wilder leapt out of the chair, sending it flying backward, long-rifle to his shoulder, aiming at the front window.

The children screamed and laughed and scrambled around to see what Tipton thought of that.

A startled George Palmer stood framed in the window. The children screamed again. Wilder rolled his eyes and lowered the gun.

"Tipton!" Wilder shouted, as much to regain the children's attention as to continue his story. They swung back to him and Wilder saw Palmer slide from view.

"'Tipton!' And here's John Sevier, Nolichucky Jack, governor of the state of Franklin. He's standing tall in the doorway next to Mrs. Brown. 'Tipton,' he says, 'I'll surrender, but not to you. I'll give myself up to Colonel Love who rides with you. But only on the condition that no harm come to Mrs. Brown.' He steps down off the porch and he's surrounded and tied up. Mrs. Brown watches Tipton's men ride away with him, heartsick, but knowing she's held her ground, she's done her part, and now it's up to others to rescue Nolichucky Jack and bring him home."

"Yippee!" a child squealed and the rest started clapping.

Wilder fielded their excited questions and let admiring eyes but no hands roam the length of the rifle. Then he turned the students over to their teacher and excused himself. He found Palmer sitting in one of the rockers on the porch.

"The Widow Brown didn't hold off Tipton's men half as well as you do, Lewis. Though don't you think the museum might be sued someday over someone's heart attack?"

"We're a non-profit organization and can't be held responsible."

"Is that true?"

"I don't know. What can I do for you?"

"I just came to get a look at Lillian's fern stand. You don't do that bit with the rifle for the senior citizens, do you?" Palmer eyed the long-rifle Wilder still cradled.

"No. Hard facts and Victorian interiors for them. I'd hate to find out I was wrong about being sued."

"Oh, I don't know, it might do one or two of them some good. Did I ever tell you about the first time I looked through that window?"

"No, was I doing something rude with one of the mannequins?"

"Not you, no, this was oh, say fifty years ago."

"Ah, before respectability slapped the place around. What were you doing looking through these windows at such an impressionable age? What were you, six, seven? I'm shocked. What was your mother thinking?"

"She had nothing to do with it and never would have known except I let it slip." Palmer gave his backside a reminiscent rub. "It was a dare. Very popular place, this was, for dares."

"I'll bet. So did you get an eyeful or were the ladies and their festivities confined to the upper rooms?"

"There was a chink in the curtains."

"Don't be racist, George."

"I've never called a gap a Chinese, but if you insist. It was just large enough for an inquiring eye. Quite an education for a seven-year-old. Hmm, well. Anyway, Lillian swears that fern stand was the perfect piece at the perfect price so I'd better take a look and then I'll be on my way."

"Whoa, stand back and let the sea of budding humanity out." Wilder held the door as twenty-five aspiring historians, or at least future vigilante riflemen, rushed through and down off the porch. The teacher and several parents were swept along with the tide. "Come, Fr. Palmer, into the calmer interior." Wilder ushered him into the smells of age and preservation, overlaced with a hint of more recent pink bubblegum.

"So, tell me Lewis, do you think it was worth the money?"

The two men stepped into a room so thoroughly Victorian it made the faint of heart fear suffocation amidst all the bedraping and bedecking. They stopped in front of the fern stand.

"Well, I've said before, I'm no expert on Victorian furniture."

"Yes, but you have some idea, don't you?"

"It looks awful enough to be the real thing. My aunt had one something like it in the attic, I think. She loathed it and I'm sure she would loathe this, too. Those are good credentials for it right there. But I wish Lillian would listen when I say we need more than just some old geezer's word for where this stuff comes from. That coffee grinder she bought might have been made in the county a hundred and fifty years ago but who knows? There's a man over in Chester…"

"You've been to Chester recently?"

"Yeah, why?"

"Didn't the Fox break into a house…"

Wilder's glare shriveled anything further along those lines Palmer might have said.

"As I was saying, there is a man in Chester who can turn out a hutch table next week that anyone would swear was made a century ago. The pieces Lillian brings in just don't mean much unless we've got some sort of documentation."

"I know it, I know it. They have no 'historical significance', as you say. But Lillian and some of the other members of the committee don't…"

"Then they shouldn't be on the Acquisitions Committee."

"Sorry, Lewis. We're all sinners and we're not the Smithsonian."

"Oh for God's sake."

"It's frustrating for you, I know, but we have to work with what we've got. Speaking of which, I'd still like you to teach that junior high Sunday school class."

"Sorry, George, it's frustrating for you, I know."

"That's all right," Palmer said, patting Wilder on the arm, "we can but try. I think you're probably right about this stand, though. If you can vouch for your aunt loathing it, then it passes muster." Palmer's eyes widened as though he'd had a revelation. He snapped his fingers. "I have a wonderful idea. Why don't you call your aunt and ask her to come look at it?"

Wilder looked sideways at Palmer. "Sorry, George, it's frustrating for you, I know."

"Someday, Lewis," Palmer said, shaking his head, "you're going to realize that taking the curator's position here in our lovely out-of-the-way town was not a successful attempt to get away from anything, but was instead a first step towards returning to something. Seventy-five miles is no distance at all and..."

"...And you've said it all before, thank you. Now, goodbye. I hear your flock bleating for you. See you Sunday." Wilder more or less pushed Palmer back out onto the porch and closed the door.

He went into the front room where the tour had finished up and glanced around to see that everything was in order. He'd left the rocking chair tipped in the corner. That was careless. He righted it and crossed over to the window to watch Palmer walking down the sidewalk back toward Main Street. He would probably stop in at Lillian's to report his pleasure with the fern stand. Yes, there he turned in at the gate. And he turned and waved back at Wilder, framed in the window. Clever bastard. Wilder liked him.

One more tour was scheduled for the afternoon but there was time before that to get something else done. He locked the rifle away. Then he walked back past the Victorian parlor, turning his head in time so he didn't have to see the fern stand again, and climbed the graceful stairway to the second floor. He paused at the door to his office thinking he ought to check on the growth rate of his mound of paperwork, but with a mental raspberry in the paperwork's direction, he opened the opposite door and climbed another set of stairs to the attic.

His first project after taking this job had been to evict the uninvited feathered guests from the attic. Then he pigeon-proofed it and vacuumed up what they'd been contributing over the years. Then he'd started in on the fun.

Inventory in one hand, hands correctly, though resentfully, clad in cotton gloves to protect whatever he touched from the insidious oils of his skin, he'd started opening boxes and pulling out drawers, shifting trunks and uncovering 'forgotten' acquisitions: a tiny pair of red leather shoes not quite worn out by a child in the 1870s; several dozen pairs of mule shoes someone had carefully cleaned and oiled and donated to the museum; clay marbles; ancient rusty black wedding suits; quilts; firearms; a firehose stiff with age; brittle photographs; newspapers; diaries; embroidery projects half-finished a century ago; a stereopticon; projectile points; broken and intact pottery, both delft and Cherokee; glass slides of a long ago trip to Egypt.

The inventory had been kept up to date only haphazardly before his arrival. That meant minor chaos for the collections but bliss for Wilder. It became his personal, protracted treasure hunt. Much protracted because he couldn't spend all his time working on it.

He flipped on the attic lights, now, filled his lungs with the still air, and smiled. He wondered if someday someone would catch him up here rubbing his hands and licking his chops.

Being the sole professional employed at the museum, Wilder kept busy juggling his various duties and spent a lot of his time working alone. But that suited him. He preferred the long stretches of solitude to the social parts of the job, though even they had a certain charm. And he'd inherited a capable staff.

Pam Sluder and Marcie Hicks spelled each other as part-time receptionists at a desk in the foyer. They welcomed visitors, answered the phone, and set up tours for groups not wanting to do the self-guided bit.

Jim Honeycutt kept the lawn mowed, the leaves raked, and the floors swept. He also lent a hand on whatever exhibit construction project might be going. He liked power tools. He loved the skill saw.

A small cadre of volunteers gave tours to students and other groups. But often Wilder had to drop his other duties and guide tours, too.

"Lewis?" Susan Peters called from the bottom of the attic stairs. Susan Peters was that godsend all museums pray for, someone trained, experienced, and reliable who could afford to volunteer her time. She came in twice a week and worked at cataloguing old photographs. "Lewis? Your tour is coming up the walk."

"They're early. Tell them to go away."

"Lewis." Susan climbed the stairs. "Stop fondling those corsets and get down there. I swear, every time I look up here you're doing something with old underwear."

"Research. This is research I'm doing for an exhibit on unmentionables."

"So long as you don't start wearing them." She disappeared again.

Wilder laid the corsets in a box lined with protective acid-free tissue. He peeled off the cotton gloves he hated. They made good museum sense but any magic in the artifacts was lost in the translation through the thin fabric. He dropped the gloves into a drawer with several other pairs and went to meet his tour.

"Are you really planning an exhibit of antique underwear?" Susan spoke to Wilder's back from the doorway of the Victorian parlor. "How long have you been standing there and what are you staring at?"

"Hm," Wilder murmured to all three questions. He remained immobile, his hands jammed in his pockets.

Susan walked around in front of Wilder and snapped her fingers under his nose. She'd told him once about her pet theory concerning the necessity of involving more than one of his senses before he could come to grips with the intricacies of logical conversation.

"What's wrong with the fern stand?"

"Nothing. It's exactly right. It's awful." He continued to be absorbed by it.

"Ah." Susan pondered the answer and the person who'd uttered it. "Well, if you do want to do an exhibit of naughty things, I've come across some photographs you might be able to use. I will tell you all this again, next time I see you, as you seem not to be here right now. I'm leaving, now. Don't bother to see me out. By the way, I'm developing a new theory, Lewis, about the psychological profile of people attracted to working in museums full time. Good bye."

Wilder flapped a hand, and remained staring at the fern stand.

"Are you locking up Lewis?" Pam looked in as she passed on her way to the door.

Wilder made an effort and roused himself.

"Yeah." He took his hands out of his pockets and with one fingertip traced the carved edge of the stand. With his other hand he rubbed the tightened muscles at the back of his neck.

The front door slammed behind Pam and Wilder went to lock it. He walked through each of the rooms downstairs, performing the evening security check, repeating the procedure upstairs, finally coming to the attic door. Something about the attic stirred in his mind. He stood there for a minute thinking. But it wasn't this attic. It was the attic of his Aunt Katherine's house.

He'd been staring at Lillian's miserable fern stand too long. A noise between a snort and a sigh stirred him. After checking to see the door was locked, he retraced his steps through the darkened museum, set the alarm, and let himself out the back way into the chilly autumn evening.

The museum made its home in a solid, square house built in the 1850s of red bricks, fired onsite, mostly by black hands. It was a typical piece of antebellum architecture, with symmetrical rows of windows up and down. Upper and lower porches with plenty of gingerbread had been added across the front in the 1880's when a traveling millwright passed through Nolichucky. By the end of World War I, though, with no one in the family left to care, the house sat empty and neglected on the hill at the northern edge of town.

In the thirties it experienced a revival of spirits when it was refurbished with several dozen rolls of flocked wallpaper and turned into a roadhouse. Most of the patrons were men from the surrounding mountains down in town for trade, gossip, and entertainment. Overnight lodging didn't cost much, and if they wanted something less wholesome and a little quicker, that was available, too.

That enterprise folded sometime in the sixties, either because the Law or the Church got the better of it, or maybe just because the roof leaked.

It took a strong-willed committee of citizens and a concerted effort at fundraising to rescue and resurrect the house as the Nolichucky Jack History Museum, dedicated to the history of the town and the area comprising the 'Lost State of Franklin.' Nolichucky Jack, formally known as John Sevier, was the governor of the lost state and subsequently the first governor of Tennessee. His colorful memory lived on at the Nolichucky Jack History Museum, and especially in the minds of those children who went through the museum on one of Lewis Wilder's livelier tours.

Wilder shivered as he walked down the brick path that ran across the lawn between the museum and the former slave quarters. The quarters, a low clapboard building, had survived as a structure through the various transitions of the big house, enjoying a few of its own along the way. In its latest incarnation, it was a perk for the museum's curator—free housing.

Wilder pulled his few pieces of mail from the box on the porch railing. More fodder for the recycling bin. It wasn't so dark yet that he stumbled up the steps or fumbled his key in the lock. He tossed the mail toward the sofa on his way past, grabbed his jacket from a peg in the kitchen, and went out the back door. He shrugged into the jacket and sat down on the steps.

"Evening, Lewis." A hat and the long handle of a garden tool were visible over a fence smothered in blackberry brambles.

"Evening, Grady," Wilder said to the hat.

"You all right?"

"Can't complain, Grady."

"Or you could, but you won't."

Wilder smiled.

Grady had introduced himself over the fence to Wilder as a compost pit philosopher. "I'm interested in all kinds of ideas," he'd told Wilder one evening soon after Wilder moved in. "I don't care where they come from. I just toss them into the compost pit of my mind and sooner or later something good grows out of it." Grady was a retired funeral home director and ex-marine. He was seventy-eight.

Wilder had listened to Grady's story in installments on fine evenings throughout the summer and fall, rarely seeing his face; sometimes surprised by the hats he wore.

"Is it broccoli or turnips tonight, Grady?"

"Cabbage."

"Cabbage."

A breeze pulled a few early red leaves off the maple in the corner of Wilder's small yard. The crickets tuned up. Grady's disembodied voice came over the fence.

"Yeah, I come out here in the evening, Lewis, and I yank up a few of the cussed weeds and I stir up my compost heap a bit. Then I plant something or I pick something."

"Are you talking about your head or your garden?"

"Garden, wise guy. I'll be picking these cabbages in February. They'll taste better than any you've ever had because they got some frost. Nothing wrong with a little nip of frost for members of the cabbage family."

Nothing wrong with a little nip of something else for the Wilder family, Wilder thought.

"I enjoy my evenings in the garden, Lewis," Grady continued. "Soothing. That's what it is. And I truly believe that if more people gardened in this world things would be different."

Wilder sat listening to the sounds of the end of the day and of the old man working in his garden. Soothing.

Grady said goodnight and Wilder went in.

The darkest part of Wilder's dreamless sleep was shattered by voices and pounding on his door.

Read Molly MacRae's "Wilder Rumors" to find out what happens next!

About Molly MacRae

Molly MacRae spent twenty years in the foothills of the Blue Ridge Mountains of Upper East Tennessee, where she managed The Book Place, an independent bookstore; may it rest in peace. Before the lure of books hooked her, she was curator of the history museum in Jonesborough, Tennessee's oldest town. Molly MacRae's first mystery novel, *Wilder Rumors*, was published in 2007. Her stories have appeared in *Alfred Hitchcock's Mystery Magazine* and she is a winner of the Sherwood Anderson Award for Short Fiction. These days, MacRae lives with her family in Champaign, Illinois, where she connects children with books at the public library.

About Darkhouse Books

Darkhouse Books is dedicated to publishing entertaining fiction, primarily in the mystery and science fiction field. Darkhouse Books is located in Niles, California, an inadvertently-preserved, 120 year old, one-sided, railtown, forty miles from San Francisco. Further information may be obtained by visiting our website at www.darkhousebooks.com.

CPSIA information can be obtained
at www.ICGtesting.com
Printed in the USA
BVOW08s1327221216
471640BV00001B/3/P

9 780990 842873